Two Sagas of Mythical Heroes

Hervor and Heidrek

&

Hrólf Kraki and His Champions

Two Sagas of Mythical Heroes

Hervor and Heidrek

&

Hrólf Kraki and His Champions

Translated and Edited, with Introduction, by

Jackson Crawford

Hackett Publishing Company, Inc.
Indianapolis/Cambridge

Copyright © 2021 by Hackett Publishing Company, Inc.

24 23 22 21   1 2 3 4 5 6 7

For further information, please address
    Hackett Publishing Company, Inc.
    P.O. Box 44937
    Indianapolis, Indiana 46244-0937

    www.hackettpublishing.com

Cover and interior design by E. L. Wilson
Photo of Jackson Crawford by Jon Wilson
Composition by Aptara, Inc.

Cataloging-in-Publication data can be accessed via the Library of Congress
Online Catalog.
Library of Congress Control Number: 2021934959

ISBN-13: 978-1-62466-995-8 (hardback)
ISBN-13: 978-1-62466-994-1 (paperback)

The paper used in this publication meets the minimum requirements of
American National Standard for Information Sciences—Permanence of Paper
for Printed Library Materials, ANSI Z39.48–1984.

∞

Contents

To Faith Ingwersen,
Standing Tree of Absaroka

Acknowledgments

I thank my students at the University of Colorado, especially Aaron Aaeng, Gabriela Abramovich, Michelle Aicega, Hussain Al Jabr, Zade Alfalah, Hesham Alsaigh, Sam Bateman, Nate Bennett, Anna Bodnar, Mallory Britz, Sarah Bustamante, Rachel Coates, Chris Creery, Lane Daigle, Graham Dean, Rachel Donati, Alienor Doremieux, Aidan Duggan, Conor Ezarik, William Fagan, Colleen Feuerborn, Michael Fruge, Sami Garner, Kelsie Gering, Calvin Good, Jacob Haimes, Toby Ann Halamka, Jacob Hans, Will Hartley, Xavier Lawrence Jackson, Aynsley Johanna Jessip, Paul Kim, Jackson Kistler, Gavriel Kleinwaks, Angela Korneev, Hayden Lewis, Heather Lewis, Lisanne Lopez-Audet, Rachel Miller, Varun Narayanswamy, Kelly Nemeth, Sylvie Novins-Montague, Steven Pearson, Candice Perrotta, Kelsey Pool, Victoria Prager, Rachel Reifsteck, Carly Romig, Elora Morgaine Root, Peter Rosenthal, Garrett Roybal, Israel Sanchez, Brian Satchell, Olivia Sidoroff, Alyson Skeens, Derek Smith, Matthew Spallas, Zachariah Talley, Alexis Thomson, Brian Tranchetti, James Tranchetti, Caitrin Wright, and Maya Yanez, for their input on these translations in the courses in which they first saw the light of day.

For their kindness, help, and friendship while this project was being completed, I thank Thomas Allen; Anouk Bachman; Robert T. Bakker; Tom Bauer; Kevin Bigley; Aleese Block; De Lane Bredvik; Gordon and Dian Bredvik; Taylor Flint Budde; Andrew and Brenna Byrd; Bodil Cappelen; Richard Cooper; Lance Cox and Averi and Scott Hoffman; Carl Day, Jenn Green, and Skylar Day; Christine Ekholst; Teresa Escalle; Kitt Euler; Nate Freeman; Kelsey Fuller; Pat Gallagher; Jason Gallmeyer; Noah Goats; Paul and Jo Ellen Gonzales; Luke Gorton; Brad Graham; Patrick Greaney; Kurt Gutjahr; Bob and Suzanne Hargis; Anne Hatfield; Karen Hawley; Merlin and Barb Heinze; Amanda Hollander; Ashraf Ismail; Bob Janke; Patrick Jones; Willie Kirby; Casey Koehler; Jimmy Lakey; Mark Leiderman; Patty Limerick; Peter and Marilyn Llewellyn; Ron and Laura Mamot; Shea McClain; Darby McDevitt; Fr. Jude McPeak; Nina Melovska; Perry Morris; Matthew T. Mossbrucker; Stella Nathaniel; Jeff Newton;

Jordan Phillips; Ryan Picazio; Brian Rak; Rob Rhiner; Lei Autumn Roberts; Simon Roper; Caley Smith; Justin Snow; Bill, Suzie, and Blake Stubblebine; Aiko Sugano; Autumn Torres; Will Tuleja; Joe and Candy Turner; Tess Van Laanen; Rob Waller; Jon Wilson; Liz Wilson; Zach Yarrow and Cara Cooper; and Donny Zwisler. I thank the staff of the Boulder Book Store for their extraordinary kindness to an unconventional local writer through four book releases. And I thank the many kind people who, with their support on Patreon for my educational video series, have allowed me to make a living from teaching.

Luke Annear and Vicki Grove deserve special thanks for their extraordinarily helpful and thorough comments on early drafts of these translations, as do the two anonymous reviewers for Hackett, who gave a generous amount of time to this project.

Finally, I thank my family, especially Katherine, Claire, Travis, Shelley, Kent, Kerri, Dad, and Mom, and the reasons why pose no riddle. Of course, I alone am responsible for all errors in these pages.

Jackson Crawford
Lake George, Colorado
April 9, 2021

Introduction

In a Nutshell

Both of the two sagas in this volume are based on ancient, pre-Christian Norse tales that survived in oral tradition for centuries before they were written down in medieval Iceland. In the case of *The Saga of Hervor and Heidrek,* these ancient roots are clear, both in the time-worn poetry spoken by its protagonists, and in the raw, archaic nature of its action and horror scenes. In the case of *The Saga of Hrólf Kraki and His Champions*—a loose collection of adventures centered around the court of the Danish king Hrólf and such legendary champions as Boðvar Little-bear—equally ancient material has been reworked in the Arthurian-inspired chivalric style popular all over Europe at the time of its writing. But each of the sagas, whatever its particular literary flavor, shares many of the characteristics that make the greatest Norse sagas such enduring favorites of medieval and modern storytellers alike: enchanted and cursed swords, the doomed courage of men and women who face death in battle with cool resolve, and the unpredictable meddling of witches and gods.

The Saga of Hervor and Heidrek: *Cast of Characters, Family Tree, and Synopsis*

Except for its final two, extraneous chapters, *The Saga of Hervor and Heidrek* is virtually a saga of the sword Tyrfing, which is mentioned in every significant incident of combat in the first fourteen chapters. The sword, which must draw blood before it is resheathed, is originally the property of a king named Sigrlami, but it is when it is in the hands of his grandson Angantýr that the action of the saga truly begins. Angantýr and his eleven brothers are berserkers, a kind of frenzied warrior who feature in many sagas, and their fate is sealed when one of them, Hjorvarð, challenges a man named Hjálmar to a battle for a

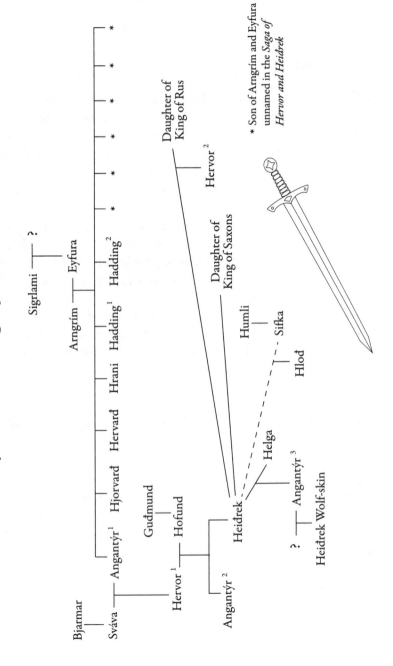

Family Tree for *The Saga of Hervor and Heiðrek*

* Son of Arngrím and Eyfura
unnamed in the *Saga of
Hervor and Heiðrek*

Swedish princess on the cursed island of Samsø. All twelve brothers are killed, and the sword Tyrfing is buried with Angantýr.

Years later, Angantýr's daughter Hervor finds out where Angantýr is buried and travels there to confront her undead father in his grave and demand the sword Tyrfing from him. The living woman and her father exchange threats in an archaic poem, usually known as *The Waking of Angantýr*, embedded in the centuries-younger text of the saga. Armed with the sword, Hervor returns home and has a son named Heiðrek. Heiðrek grows up to father three children with a succession of wives and concubines, and becomes a powerful king. Before the end of his reign, Heiðrek answers the riddles of the god Óðin delivered in another embedded poem known as *The Riddles of Gestumblindi*.

Following the death of King Heiðrek, his son Angantýr succeeds him. Heiðrek's illegitimate Hunnish son Hloð soon appears at Angantýr's court demanding half of the inheritance from Heiðrek, which Angantýr denies him, leading to battle. Angantýr's sister Hervor, a warrior like her grandmother, dies in an early skirmish before Angantýr and Hloð face off directly. It the end, Angantýr kills his half-brother Hloð and utters a famous stanza about the injustice of his own, and his half-brother's, fate. Much of the action of this part of the saga is extrapolated from, or quoted from, a very archaic poem referred to in Old Norse as *Hlǫðskviða* "Hloð's Poem" but in English usually called *The Battle of the Goths and Huns*.

The Saga of Hrólf Kraki and His Champions: *Cast of Characters, Family Tree, and Synopsis*

The Saga of Hrólf Kraki and His Champions is a much more chaotically organized text than *The Saga of Hervor and Heiðrek*. While it loosely follows the fortunes of the ancient Danish royal family known as the Skjoldungs, from King Hálfdan to his grandson King Hrólf, it is full of digressions about the champions at King Hrólf's court, and even about the families of these champions, which takes up a great deal of space and creates an impression of a storyteller trying to include everything he knows about anyone connected to the central characters.

Family Tree for *The Saga of Hrólf Kraki*

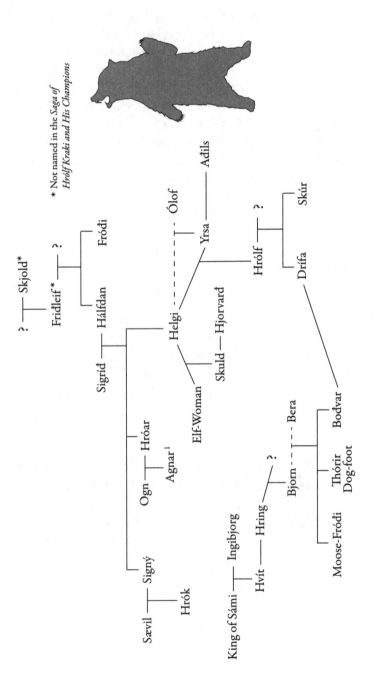

* Not named in the *Saga of Hrólf Kraki and His Champions*

The saga is broken up into seven "parts" or "tales" (Old Norse *þættir,* literally "threads"). Part 1 ("The Tale of Fróði") comprises chapters 1–5 and tells of the vengeance that the young Danish princes Hróar and Helgi take for their father Hálfdan on their wicked uncle Fróði. Part 2 ("The Tale of Helgi") comprises chapters 6–17 and tells of how Helgi rose to be king of Denmark. During his reign, he rapes Queen Ólof of Saxony and then unknowingly marries their daughter Yrsa and has a son named Hrólf with her (he also has a daughter, named Skuld, with an "elf-woman"). When Helgi's wife Yrsa discovers she is also his daughter, she leaves him and subsequently is married to King Aðils of Sweden, who lures Helgi under false pretenses to Sweden and has him killed there.

Part 3 ("The Tale of Svipdag"), chapters 18–23, tells the origin of the Swedish hero Svipdag and his brothers, and how they serve first with King Aðils of Sweden before leaving him to join the court of King Hrólf, Helgi's son and heir to the throne of Denmark. Part 4 ("The Tale of Boðvar"), chapters 24–36, tells the memorable story of the Norwegian hero Boðvar "Little-bear" and his half-animal brothers, the sons of a man cursed to spend his days as a bear. Like Svipdag before him, Boðvar sails south to Denmark and joins the court of King Hrólf, following a fight with a monster that bears a strong resemblance to Beowulf's fight with Grendel and no doubt shares a common origin with that Old English legend. Part 5 ("The Tale of Hjalti"), chapter 37, is only nominally focused on the hero Hjalti, who begins life as an abused young boy rescued by Boðvar and is later turned into a fierce warrior by drinking a monster's blood. Part 6 ("Concerning Aðils, King at Uppsala, and King Hrólf's Journey to Sweden with His Champions"), chapters 38–46, chronicles Hrólf Kraki's journey to Sweden to avenge his father Helgi on King Aðils, and the encounters he has on the way to and from with the god Óðin in disguise. In Part 7 ("Concerning the Battle with Skuld, and the Fall of King Hrólf and His Champions"), chapters 47–52, years after returning victorious to Denmark, Hrólf is attacked and defeated by the army of his sister Skuld in a final battle marked by strange, long speeches, the appearance of Boðvar (like his father before him) in the form of a bear, and a remarkably "loud" narrative voice that dwells in long paragraphs on the virtues of Hrólf and his champions and the shame of their lack of Christian faith.

The internal consistency and narrative continuity between these parts or tales is often weak. For example, in chapter 49, near the beginning of Part 7, Bodvar Little-bear is introduced with a brief retelling of his story, as though he were a new character and not one of the most memorable actors in the saga since chapter 27. By contrast, King Hrólf's sword Skofnung is treated as an important attribute of his that must already be familiar to the reader from the first time it is abruptly mentioned in chapter 45.

Ancient Stories, Medieval Sagas

Like *The Saga of the Volsungs* (see *The Saga of the Volsungs with The Saga of Ragnar Lothbrok*, Hackett, 2017), neither of these sagas represents an undiluted transmission of legends from the Viking Age, but rather a refraction of those legendary materials through the literary and linguistic lens of the later Middle Ages when they were written down.

In the case of *The Saga of Hrólf Kraki and His Champions*, this writing occurred during the 1400s AD, a time when a style heavily influenced by Arthurian romance was popular everywhere in Catholic Europe, including in Iceland. Thus, while the kernel of Hrólf's story surely is even older than the Viking Age (to judge from the oblique references to some of its characters in *Beowulf*, a poem composed between AD 800 and 1000), he and his champions are seen strutting their horses in knightly magnificence when they approach King Adils's city.

Contrasting with the neutral presentation of pre-Christian ideas and rites in *The Saga of the Volsungs* is this saga author's attitude toward the earlier pagan religion of Scandinavia. Consider the conclusion of chapter 48 of *The Saga of Hrólf Kraki and His Champions*:

> And it is not told anywhere that King Hrólf or his champions sacrificed to the gods at any time, but rather that they believed in their own strength and abilities. This was because, at the time, the holy faith had not been preached yet here in the Northlands, and thus the men who dwelled in the northern part of the world still had little knowledge of their Creator.

Not only is the polytheistic pre-Christian religion dismissed in this passage, but the heroes of the story (not observant of noticeably Christian virtues) are emphatically described as what the authors of the earlier Sagas of Icelanders called "godless men." These were not atheists, but rather men who lived in a time before Christianity came to the north and yet rejected the worship of their contemporaries' gods. King Hrólf even calls Óđin, chief of the Norse gods—and a being he personally encounters in the flesh!—"an evil spirit" (ch. 46). Such a man, if he encounters missionaries of the new religion, is sure to accept it, but as the narrative voice of this saga even admonishes the hero directly in chapter 52: "One thing prevented your victory, King Hrólf, that you did not know your Creator."

Nonetheless, traces of the old beliefs, or at least of the language of the old beliefs, show through at different points in *The Saga of Hrólf Kraki and His Champions*. In chapter 51, only one chapter previous to the one in which the narrator scolds Hrólf for his lack of faith, his hero Hjalti comments encouragingly that he and his fellows will be guests in Óđin's hall, Valhalla, after their deaths—a fitting reward in the afterlife for a slain Viking warrior.

In *The Saga of Hervor and Heidrek,* the echoes of the deeper past ring much louder. Most famously, the place name given as *Harvađafjǫll* "*Harvađa*-mountains" in one stanza of *The Battle of the Goths and Huns* must go back to the name of the Carpathian Mountains, Greek *karpátēs,* as transmitted to a Germanic language before these languages had undergone the consonant shift known as Grimm's Law, in which an older [k] became [h], and older [p] and [t] eventually became (in unstressed position, as here) [v] and [ð], respectively. This sound change was completed long before the first attestations of a Germanic language in writing (ca. AD 160), and so the presence of this name testifies to much earlier contact between Scandinavians (or perhaps Goths or other peoples speaking closely related languages) and Greek-speakers than is otherwise in evidence.[1]

---

1. The profound resemblance of the earliest form of the runic alphabet, the Elder Futhark, to certain provincial variants of the Greek alphabet, might also point to contact with Greeks (or an intermediary culture with close Greek contacts) at an earlier date than otherwise documented. See Richard L. Morris's study, *Runic and Mediterranean Epigraphy* (Odense University Press, 1988).

The Saga of Hervor and Heidrek is known from three important Icelandic manuscripts and their later copies. The well-known *Hauksbók* (ca. AD 1300), which also contains a variety of other texts that intersect with Norse mythology (including a version of the Eddic poem *Vǫluspá*), has an incomplete copy of the saga, called the "H-"text, which is the oldest known written text of this saga (*Hauksbók* is preserved in fragments; *Hervor* is contained in the part catalogued as AM 544 4to, beginning on p. 72v). Unfortunately, as with other texts in that manuscript (such as *The Saga of Eirík the Red*), the text of *The Saga of Hervor and Heidrek* in *Hauksbók* is poorly edited, as if the scribe had worked under orders to abridge its length but had no clear idea of where to make cuts. Most scholars consider the "R-"text, in the manuscript catalogued as GKS 2845 4to (ca. AD 1400s), which also lacks the ending of the saga, to be the best-preserved version of the text as far as it goes. A third manuscript (known as the "U-"text), produced in the 1600s and now lost, is known from two early copies and is the only source for much of the latter part of the saga. The U- and H-texts are nearer to one another in wording than either is to the R-text, which is the usual basis of printed editions and translations, including this one.

The Saga of Hrólf Kraki and His Champions is later and known only from late manuscripts (the oldest surviving text was written no earlier than the 1630s). It was apparently very popular in the early modern period, as manuscripts are numerous, and versions from that era are found containing not only the original Old Norse text but sometimes a Latin translation of it as well. Five manuscripts of the Old Norse text, mostly written between 1650 and 1700, are considered important by modern philologists and do not differ significantly in the text they present;[2] all five are probably copies from a single lost Icelandic manuscript produced shortly before 1600.

---

2. These five are the manuscripts catalogued as AM 285 4to; AM 109a 8vo; Sth. Papp. 4to nr. 17; AM 9 fol.; and the oldest, AM 11 fol. Desmond Slay produced an exhaustive study of the numerous manuscripts of this saga in *The Manuscripts of Hrólfs saga kraka* (Munksgaard, 1960).

Literary Style

Both of these sagas share some literary characteristics with other Icelandic sagas, namely the often sudden vacillation between the narration and a line of direct dialogue, with no transition, as in this excerpt from chapter 19 of *The Saga of Hrólf Kraki and His Champions:*

> King Adils now told Svipdag not to serve the king's interests any less than all the berserkers had together, "Especially because the queen wants you to serve in the place of the berserkers." So Svipdag remained there for a time.

Another example may be seen in chapter 2 of *The Saga of Hervor and Heidrek:*

> "Each of these two men is so great and from such a good family," he said, that he couldn't deny his daughter to either of them, and he asked his daughter to choose which one she wanted to have.

Another characteristic of Icelandic saga literature is the web of relationships that the narrator seems to assume the audience can easily remember. Characters are often introduced with large numbers of relations, close and distant, who may suddenly appear in later chapters with little or no introduction or refresher at that point. Living in a society that prized family ties, it may be that the medieval Norse audience did not struggle to remember such networks of relations, but for the modern reader the effect is often jarring and calls for family trees and glossaries of names such as those printed in this volume.

The Saga of Hrólf Kraki and His Champions shows an especially marked predilection for hendiadys, repeating the same thing in two different ways as a means of emphasis: "burning everything and setting it to the torch" (ch. 1), "every danger and conflict" (ch. 16), "such beautiful and lovely women as they were" (ch. 24), "arrogant and proud" (ch. 25).

From the perspective of the reader of Old Norse, the vocabulary, grammar, and many idiomatic phrases of *The Saga of Hrólf Kraki and His Champions* will also make the impression of a late stage of the language, well on its way toward Modern Icelandic. An example of this is in chapter 1, when Vífill says in the original, *Hér er við ramman reip at draga,* literally, "Here's a strong rope to pull against," an expression derived from the great popularity of tug-of-war games in early modern Iceland and most effectively translated as simply, "Here is a difficult task." Noticeably late vocabulary includes the use of *geta* to mean "can, be able," and the use of *hvaða* (rather than *hverr*) as the interrogative or indefinite pronominal adjective "which, what" (e.g., *hvaða sveinar þeir væri,* "what boys they might be," ch. 3).

Other stylistic features of this saga probably owe something to the popularity of new and foreign models of storytelling that had begun to be absorbed by saga writers in later medieval Iceland. Earlier sagas had seldom if ever dealt in the internal monologue of their characters, and were apt to present both sides in a deadly rivalry as realistic men with conflicting interests—often with the best men from both sides of a conflict forced to kill one another for the sake of their family ties or sworn word. But influenced by the style of chivalric Europe, *The Saga of Hrólf Kraki and His Champions* is quite different, with competent, elaborately praised heroes arrayed against feeble, scheming villains who almost seem to twist their mustaches with glee as they carry out their evil deeds, as here in chapter 41:

> It was done as he ordered, and he wanted to be sure where King Hrólf was, because he thought that he would not be able to stand the heat as well as his champions, and he thought that it would be easier to seize him if he knew where he was, because he truly wanted King Hrólf dead.

Or in chapter 48, where we see the narrator going to unnecessary, pompous lengths to aggrandize his heroes:

> He [King Hrólf] was thinking more about his own grandeur and magnanimity and propriety, and about all of the courage that dwelled in his own heart. And he was eager to serve everyone who came, and his good reputation traveled far and wide, and he had every single thing that a king of this world might need to adorn his pride.

This may sound strange to a reader accustomed to the style of other Icelandic sagas, though not to that of, for example, *The Saga of Amícus and Amilíus*, a knight's story probably translated into Old Norse from Low German about the same time as *The Saga of Hrólf Kraki and His Champions* was written down. There, too, the evil thoughts of duplicitous characters (especially women) are transparent to the narrator and the audience.

Also differing from the usually more terse style of Icelandic sagas (well exemplified in much of *Hervor* or *Volsungs*) is the large amount of meandering speeches in *Hrólf,* not only by the characters but by the narrator as well. These speeches mount in number as the end of the saga approaches, and by chapter 50 we have an example such as this, which King Hrólf Kraki launches into in the midst of battle:

> King Hrólf said, "He must be somewhere, and I'm sure it's somewhere that benefits us, as long as he has a say in it. Keep up your dignity and keep up your attack, and don't slander him—not any one of you is equal to him. However, I don't mean to scold any of you, because you are all among the most valorous of men."

Parallels in Other Sources

Hrólf Kraki must have been an exceptionally well-known legendary hero in the medieval period, with the number of references to him elsewhere in Old Norse literature eclipsed only by references to the heroes of the Volsung family.

A short version of many of the same events as told in *The Saga of Hrólf Kraki and His Champions* is found in *Ynglinga saga*, "The Saga of the Ynglings," the first constituent saga in Snorri Sturluson's series of sagas about the Norwegian kings called *Heimskringla*. Here, King Aðils is introduced as a warlike Swedish king who takes Yrsa, daughter of Queen Álof of Saxony, back home with him after a raid. King Helgi of Denmark raids Aðils's own kingdom in Sweden later, and in turn Helgi takes Yrsa home as his own bride. After they have had a son named Hrólf Kraki, Yrsa learns that she is her new husband Helgi's own daughter, and returns to Aðils in Sweden. Helgi dies in battle (though not in Sweden), and eventually his son, the new king Hrólf

Kraki, finds himself in Sweden, where he "sowed gold at Fýrisvellir" (though nothing more is told of that expedition, nor of its cause or resolution). Hrólf Kraki dies later at his capital Lejre, though how is not told. This abridged version is close enough in general profile, and distinct enough in some details, to suggest that Snorri knew a version of Hrólf Kraki's story preserved in lost poems or sagas that did not entirely agree with the one in the saga preserved today.

Two versions of the story of the magical millstone Grotti, known from the Eddic poem *Grottasǫngr* and from Snorri Sturluson's *Prose Edda* respectively, also include some alternative details about the early generations of Hrólf Kraki's family. In Snorri's brief account of the tale (which is quoted as a preface to the poem in *The Poetic Edda: Stories of the Norse Gods and Heroes*, Hackett, 2015), it is a "sea-king named Mysing" who kills Fróði at the end of his long and peaceful reign, rather than his nephews who kill him in his burning hall.

The poem *Grottasǫngr* itself, however, tells a story closer to the saga; there, the giant-women who work the millstone foresee (in st. 22) that it is Hálfdan's son who will kill Fróði. The text of the poem in Old Norse does not name the son, though it names his mother Yrsa, and implies that the son is Hrólf Kraki, as this stanza includes the strange facts of Hrólf's origins as narrated also in the saga: "He will be called / his mother's son / and also her brother, / we both know that." This appears to be (from the perspective of *The Saga of Hrólf Kraki and His Champions*) a conflation between Hrólf Kraki and his father Helgi, as Helgi was Hálfdan's son in the saga, and he both fathered Yrsa and fathered his son Hrólf Kraki with her.

Further afield, in the famous Old English poem *Beowulf*, the Danish king Healfdene (= Old Norse *Hálfdan*) has three sons, Heorogār, Hrōðgār (= *Hróarr*[3]), and Halga (= *Helgi*); they and their dynasty are called *Scyldingas* (= *Skjǫldungar*). While in *Beowulf* it is the uncle

---

3. When a Norse name occurs in narrative, or when I am discussing a *character*, I write the name using the anglicization rules explained in "A Note on Language and Spelling," below. The most visible change in so doing is the removal of the *-r* at the end of most men's names and some women's names, so that I usually write Hrólf (not Hrólfr), Hróar (not Hróarr), Hlod (not Hlǫðr). But when I discuss these names as names per se, I use the conventional Old Norse spellings (Hrólfr, Hróarr, Hlǫðr). Where these Old Norse spellings differ from the more anglicized spelling used in the narrative, they are given in parentheses after the applicable name in the Glossary.

Hrōðgār/Hróar who rules when his hall is invaded by a monster, and in the Icelandic saga it is the nephew Hrōðulf/Hrólf, in both stories it is a non-Danish visitor from the north, Beowulf or Boðvar Little-bear, who (after receiving a rude welcome from some of the Danes, but not from the king) subdues the creature. And given that the name *Beowulf* "bee-wolf" has been interpreted as a poetic name for "bear" (bears and wolves are both predatory animals, but the "wolf" that attacks beehives is a bear), it is interesting to note that Boðvar Little-bear is the son of a bear, and turns into a bear in his final fight much later in the saga.

In considering the history of the legendary Danish dynasty of the *Skjǫldungar*, the Icelandic saga and *Beowulf* are nearly photo-negatives of one another. *The Saga of Hrólf Kraki and His Champions* has little to say of Hróar (Old English *Hrōðgār*) in his adulthood; after the tale of Helgi and Hróar's vengeance for their father, Hróar fades quickly into the background, eventually dying as king of some part of England (not Denmark, as in *Beowulf*). In direct contrast, *Beowulf* has very little to say of his nephew Hrōðulf (Old Norse *Hrólfr*), the central protagonist of the Icelandic telling. In *Beowulf*, Hrōðulf lives with his uncle Hrōðgār in his court at Heorot in Denmark, though the poem darkly hints that perhaps their peace was spoiled later (*þā gyt wæs hiera sib ætgædere, / ǣghwylċ ōðrum trȳwe*, we read in lines 1164–65 when Hrōðgār and Hrōðulf drink together: "At this time their kinship was still intact, / each true to the other"). These hints seem to be confirmed when Hrōðgār's own queen, Wealhthēo, pleadingly toasts her nephew Hrōðulf for the kindness she trusts him to show her children when Hrōðgār dies.

Considering the distance of time and space between *Beowulf* and *The Saga of Hrólf Kraki and His Champions*—the pens that first wrote them were separated by one thousand miles of the North Atlantic and four to six centuries—the broad agreements in names, relations, and even scenes are surprisingly close. That different characters in the same family tree are emphasized, or that different strangers from across the sea vanquish the monster terrorizing the ruling family's hall, are exactly the kind of minor divergences expected with so many intervening generations passing the story on in Iceland and England, respectively.

The Danish historian Saxo Grammaticus, in book 2 of his Latin *Gesta Danorum* (*History of the Danes*) from approximately AD 1200, is another medieval source that relates the story of King Hrólf (*Rolvo* in his Latin text) in similar but not identical details to those of the Icelandic saga. Like the saga, Saxo tells that King *Helgo* (Helgi) had a daughter named *Ursa* (Yrsa) who was produced by rape, though as he tells it, the rape was of a virgin named Thora rather than of a queen. Subsequently, Thora instructs Ursa to sleep with Helgo in revenge, and the child of that union is Rolvo. After Rolvo has become king, his mother Ursa marries the Swedish king *Athislus* (Aðils). Rolvo visits them in Sweden at one point, where he boasts of his great physical endurance and is made to prove it by standing very close to a large open fire (reminding one of the tests that both Aðils and Óðin subject Hrólf and his men to in the Icelandic saga). Rolvo is awarded with many treasures by Athislus for undergoing this test.

Ursa and Rolvo then steal a great deal of treasure from Athislus and flee Sweden, with Ursa coming up with the idea to strew the ground behind them with treasure. Here, as in the Icelandic saga, Athislus himself stops to pick up a particular item, but in this source it is a heavy ornamental collar that he has previously awarded to Rolvo.

Boðvar Bjarki and Hjalti also make an appearance in Saxo's telling, as *Biarco* and *Hialto*. Like in the Icelandic saga, some of Rolvo's men throw bones at Hialto during a feast, but instead of his valiant protector, Biarco is simply a man accidentally hit by one of the bones intended for Hialto, and he throws it back and injures the man who threw it. A brawl then breaks out between Hialto and Biarco on the one hand and the remaining feasters on the other, during which for no apparent reason a bear appears in the midst of the fight for Biarco to kill. Biarco instructs Hialto to drink its blood in order to become stronger.

Saxo also relates his own version of another story in the saga, telling of a certain poor Wiggo who gives King Rolvo his nickname (*kraki* or "pole-ladder") in a casual aside and is then rewarded for this "name-giving" with great treasure. Wiggo, as does his analogue *Vogg* in the saga, then pledges his fealty to Rolvo in exchange and swears to avenge his death.

Also as in the saga, Rolvo later has his sister *Sculda* (Skuld) married to one of his governors, *Hiarwarthus* (Hjarvarð). Hiarwarthus leads a coup against Rolvo, at the start of which Hialto is amorously entangled with his lover. She asks him how old of a man she ought to marry if Hialto dies, a question that Hialto answers by cutting off her nose and telling her to decide for herself. Hialto then wakes Biarco and the other champions of Rolvo with a series of poetic lines in Latin (to which Biarco responds with some of his own) that likely go back to a lost Old Norse poem putatively titled *Bjarkamál* "words of/for (Boðvar) Bjarki."

They lose the battle, and Rolvo and almost all of his warriors die. At the victory feast that follows, the sole survivor of Rolvo's loyal men, Wiggo, kills Hiarwarthus in vengeance for him after pretending to consider swearing him fealty. In a curious postscript, Saxo adds in Book 3 of *Gesta Danorum* that Rolvo's old enemy Athislus died of alcohol poisoning from drinking too much at a funeral feast he threw in Rolvo's honor back in Sweden.

Saxo also knew a version of the story related in the saga's first chapters, in which Fróði kills his brother Hálfdan, and this is avenged by Hálfdan's son Helgi, but in Saxo's version Helgi is unconnected to the Helgi who is Hrólf's father, and the story is told in chapter 7 of *Gesta Danorum* in a context unrelated to the Hrólf Kraki narrative (which is in chapter 2 of *Gesta Danorum*).

Back in Iceland, Hrólf Kraki's sword Skofnung makes an appearance in some manuscripts of *The Saga of Kormák*, one of the classic sagas of the Icelandic warrior-poets known as the *skálds*. In this saga, Kormák is loaned the sword before a duel, and he is instructed that it has a magical snake that lives inside of it; Kormák must care for this snake in an elaborate manner in order for the sword to serve him well. However, Kormák disregards these instructions and mistreats the snake, negating the sword's unspecified magical powers. Later (in the chronology of the saga narratives themselves), the sword appears in *The Saga of the People of Laxárdal*, where it is an important heirloom of the powerful Thorkel in the saga's latest chapters. Thorkel carries Skofnung together with a magical stone, which is the only means to heal an injury given by the sword. Following Thorkel's death at sea, the sword mysteriously "survives" him and washes up on an island later called

"Skofnung Island." In both of these sagas, the sword is explicitly the same as the one in *Hrólf,* and was at some unspecified point *tekinn ór haugi Hrólfs kraka* ("taken out of the burial mound of Hrólf Kraki," according to *Laxardál,* ch. 78).

The events and characters of *The Saga of Hervor and Heiðrek* have fewer parallels in other sources, but the fight on Samsø in chapter 3, between Angantýr and his brothers on the one hand, and Arrow-Odd and Hjálmar on the other, must have been a well-known and ancient tale. It is told in nearly identical language in chapter 14 of *The Saga of Arrow-Odd,* though with an expanded focus on Arrow-Odd's preparations for the battle and his burial of the other participants afterward. In fact, the unanimous agreement of the combatants that the survivor(s) will bury the fallen with their weapons unplundered is a major plot point in *Arrow-Odd,* and though it is unmentioned in *Hervor,* it was a detail presumably known to its author (given that the sword Tyrfing must be left in Angantýr's grave for his daughter Hervor to take much later). Curiously, *Arrow-Odd* also provides names for more of Angantýr's brothers than *Hervor.*[4]

Another, very abbreviated, version of the story of the fight on Samsø is preserved in Saxo Grammaticus's *History of the Danes,* Book 5. Here, the fight is the product of a chance meeting between the hostile parties, when both "Hialmerus" and "Arvaroddus" (a Latinized form of *Qrvar-Oddr,* "Arrow-Odd") and their enemies, the twelve sons of "Arngrimus," encounter each other there when the latter are raiding.[5] As in the other versions, "Arvaroddus" is the only survivor, but here he defeats his enemies by beating them to death with a ship's rudder.

Outside of the vast heroic literature preserved in Old Norse, the small remnants of Old English heroic poetry suggest that stories preserved in *Hervor* were known in England too; the Old English poem

4. The names of the twelve brothers given there are Hervarð, Hjorvarð, Hrani, Angantýr, Bíld, Búi, Barri, Tóki, Tind, Tyrfing, and two named Hadding. Twin brothers named Hadding or something similar are known elsewhere in Norse literature, including another pair who are allies of Hjálmar and Arrow-Odd in the same *The Saga of Arrow-Odd.* It is also intriguing to see Angantýr's sword's name Tyrfing given here to a brother of his. The *Hauksbók* text of *Hervor* gives similar names.
5. Saxo gives the names of the twelve brothers here as Brander, Biarbi, Brodder, Hiarrandi, Tander, Tirvingar, duo Haddingi ("two Hadding's"), Hiorwarth, Hiarwarth, Rani, Angantir, thus closely approaching the list given in *Arrow-Odd.*

Widsið includes a *Heaðoric* (= Old Norse *Heiðrekr*) in a list of famous kings of Goths and Huns in the past. Other names mentioned here are *Sifeca* (= Old Norse *Sifka*), *Hliðe* (similar to Old Norse *Hlǫðr*), *Incgenþeow* (similar to Old Norse *Angantýr*), and *Wyrmhere* (= Old Norse *Ormarr*, "worm-warrior"). Given the very archaic language and certain telling peculiarities of meter[6] in the poems of *Hervor*, especially *The Battle of the Goths and the Huns*, plus the subject matter of Gothic kings such as Heiðrek and Angantýr, it is also probable (but unverifiable) that parts of the action of at least the latter half of the saga go back to stories brought northward from Gothic-speaking lands at the end of the Roman Empire to their linguistic cousins in Scandinavia.

There is also a possibility that two names in *The Saga of Hervor and Heiðrek* are connected to two historical Gothic tribes' names: the name of the sword Tyrfing to the people known as the Tervingi and the name of the Grýting tribe to the people known as the Greutungi. While the means by which these names survived and became applied as they are in the saga cannot be known with certainty, their presence suggests further links with a very deep past for parts of this saga, potentially reaching back into a fundamentally real (though heavily distorted) history of the warfare of Gothic and Hunnish tribes in the waning days of the Roman Empire.

Men and Women in the Sagas

The relationships between men and women, and the roles taken by men and women, in the two sagas in this volume are at once both demonstrative of the norms of medieval Norse society and of striking deviations from those norms.

While it is misleading to describe medieval Norse society as feminist, it is striking that the saga with more foreign, chivalric influence is also the one with a more contemptuous view of women. In *The Saga of Hrólf Kraki and His Champions*, the sexes are at war, with men

---

6. The observable unevenness in line length within the poem can be attributed to the loss of unaccented syllables from some words, which occurred as the poem was passed down with its original wording even as the language was undergoing significant changes in subsequent centuries.

decidedly getting the upper hand in imposing their will, and women reduced to subterfuge and magic (for both of which they are condemned) in order to have any chance of imposing theirs. The overall tone of their meetings is reminiscent of those stanzas of *Hávamál* in which the god Óðin observes that "Faithlessness is planted at their [women's] core" (st. 84) but equally that "I know both men and women: / men lie to women" (st. 91).

In chapter 7 of *The Saga of Hrólf Kraki and His Champions,* we are introduced to Queen Ólof of Saxony, who "led her life in the way of war-kings" (*hon var á þá leið sem herkonungar*). The narrator in this chapter seems to vacillate rapidly between disapproving of her unconventional lifestyle ("she was beautiful in appearance, but grim and arrogant in behavior") and regarding her as an unusually desirable woman ("It was said by men that, of all women anyone had heard tell of during that time in the Northlands, she would be the best choice in marriage, but she wanted to marry no man."). By chapter 13, the news that she has married her daughter Yrsa to Yrsa's own father, King Helgi, results in Yrsa's remark that Ólof is "the worst and the cruelest of all mothers," without a moment's mention of Helgi's own violent rape of Ólof, which Ólof had sought to avenge by arranging this marriage.

Helgi's later relationships with women are no less marked by force. When, in chapter 15, he is visited by an elf-woman whose looks he likes, he tells her she has no choice in whether or not she will sleep with him. The woman submits ("It is yours to decide, lord") but leaves the next day with instructions as to how Helgi is to meet the child conceived in this meeting two years later. The encounter ends only with a note that Helgi is more cheerful than he had been previously.

When Hjalti, nicknamed "the Righteous" (*inn hugprúði*) bites off a woman's nose for her answer to a poorly worded question in chapter 49, the modern reader recoils in horror. But the narrator quickly moves on from the scene, and does not cease to call Hjalti by his "Righteous" nickname. In fact, this is fairly consistent with the contemptuous portrayal of women who are even suspected of infidelity in knightly literature in medieval Europe. In *Mǫttuls saga,* for example, an Icelandic version of a tale widespread in European chivalric literature, a cloak made by an "elf-woman" (*álfkona*) is brought in what the saga calls "a strange and entertaining incident" (*kynligum ok gamans-amligum atburð*) to King Arthur's court. The mantle publicly demonstrates the infidelity of each woman who tries it on by becoming either too short or too long for her to wear (though it looks perfectly sized before it is tried on). The final woman who tries it on is the only one who has been faithful, and she cheerfully acknowledges as legitimate the rage that the men direct at all the other women.

Meanwhile, the depiction of women in *The Saga of Hervor and Heiðrek* is almost the opposite of what is seen in *The Saga of Hrólf Kraki and His Champions*. Two of the most famous examples of warrior-women in Old Norse literature are the two women named Hervor, a grandmother and granddaughter, in this saga. While the warrior-woman (or in Old Norse, *skjaldmær*, "shieldmaiden") is a stock figure in Norse sagas, typically she is either a two-dimensional figure (such as Ólof in *The Saga of Hrólf Kraki and His Champions*) or a woman who takes up arms on only one occasion (such as Guðrún in *The Saga of the Volsungs*, who fights alongside her brothers in their last stand). The two Hervors are truly unique in Old Norse literature for the way combat defines their lives and characters. While the Valkyries of Norse mythology share their desire to be present in battles, and many supernatural "giant" (*jǫtunn*) women, such as Skaði, freely defy gender norms and wear men's weapons and armor, the Hervors are mortal human women whose routine warlike behavior is not condemned by the narrator, but instead seems to make them unusually desirable and praiseworthy.

Even the men in the saga—excepting Bjarmar, the maternal grandfather of the first Hervor, early on—seem to approve of the women's martial lifestyles. Hofund, in chapter 5, actually seems particularly attracted to Hervor after learning this part of her story. Although it is not likely that such literary characters represent a common lifestyle for real women during the Viking Age, there is some debatable archaeological evidence for women fighters in the form of the graves of women buried with weapons of war (such as the famous Bj.581 grave from Birka in Sweden).[7] More directly, the Hervors show us that the early

---

7. The grave Bj.581 is a particularly striking example, because it was excavated in 1878 and has remained famous ever since as a splendid example of a wealthy (male) warrior's grave. When twenty-first-century science revealed that the skeletal remains were in fact

xxviii   *Introduction*

Norse did not find it inconceivable or ridiculous that a woman might aspire to live outside of a narrowly defined range of roles, an open-mindedness that seems suppressed in the later, chivalric *Saga of Hrólf Kraki and His Champions.*

Poems of the Sagas

While both of these sagas preserve poetry, it is striking that *The Saga of Hrólf Kraki and His Champions* preserves so little, given that the characters and scenes memorialized in this saga are referenced in some very old poems preserved outside the saga. For example, poems by Eyvind skáldaspillir ("Eyvind the Plagiarist," died ca. AD 990) and Thjódólf Arnórsson (died 1066) mention events from the fight at Fýrisvellir (ch. 45).

One of the poems in *The Saga of Hervor and Heidrek,* called *Hervararkviða* ("Hervor's Poem") in Old Norse and usually *The Waking of Angantýr* in English translation, was the first Eddic poem ever translated into English, by clergyman and early linguistic scholar George Hickes in 1705. Before the explosion of interest in all things Viking in the twentieth century, this poem (in a variety of different translations) was one of the few examples of genuine Old Norse literature well-known to the reading public in the English language.

The poem quoted in pieces across chapters 11–14, often called *Hlǫðskviða* ("Hlod's Poem") or *The Battle of the Goths and Huns* when printed outside the context of the saga, is among the oldest known poems in Old Norse, potentially older than even the very archaic *Atlakviða* and *Hamðismál* in the Poetic Edda.

Both of these long poems are in the meter called *fornyrðislag* "old sayings meter," the meter also used in most of the narrative poems of the Poetic Edda (see Seiichi Suzuki's work, in the Further Reading section, for an in-depth review of the characteristics of this and other Old Norse meters). Note that the meters of Eddic poetry in Old Norse

---

those of a woman, a vigorous and ongoing debate in the scholarly community erupted over what this might mean for the woman's status in life. Scholars today disagree over whether she was herself a war leader, or perhaps, for example, buried with tributes left to her by prominent male relatives.

rarely require a fixed number of syllables or a fixed rhythmic pattern (in contrast with well-known meters in traditional English poetry, such as iambic pentameter or tetrameter). Instead, each line will have a certain number of stressed syllables that are counted as "lifts," with the number determined by the specific meter, and a certain pattern of alliteration among the lifts.

A lift must be a syllable with primary or secondary stress. Unlike the less predictable situation in English, all words in Old Norse have their primary stress on the first syllable, and only the first syllable of a word may take part in alliteration.

A typical *fornyrðislag* stanza consists of eight lines, with each odd line joined to the following even line by alliteration. Each line will have two lifts (less often one) and one to four other syllables (rarely zero or up to six); at least one of the lifts in the odd line alliterates with at least one of the lifts in the following even line. There is no coordination between the alliteration in one couplet and the next. An example is the famous last stanza of *Hloðskviða*, uttered by Angantýr, printed here in the original Old Norse with a slash above each lift and with the first letter of each alliterating lift underlined (note that any vowel alliterates with any other vowel):

>   /   /
> Bǫlvat er okkr, bróðir,
>   /   /
> bani em ek þinn orðinn.
>   / /
> Þat mun enn uppi,
>   /   /
> illr er dómr norna.

As seen in this example, very often the first syllable of the even line is an alliterating lift, and typically the second lift in the even line does not participate in alliteration.

While Old Norse meters can be successfully imitated in original English compositions, Old Norse is a much more "compact" medium of expression than English overall, requiring fewer words to express

the same thought, because the language uses a rich system of inflec-
tional endings and vowel mutations to indicate the relationships of
words to one another. Old Norse also has no indefinite article (English
a, an), and the archaic language of these old poems makes little use
even of the definite article (English *the*), so these words require extra
space in the line in English. Because I favor communicating the meaning of an Old Norse stanza over compromising its meaning to preserve
its form, I have therefore made it my practice to translate Old Norse
poems into rhythmic free verse in English.

The riddles in *The Saga of Hervor and Heidrek* are often collectively
referred to as a poem under the title *The Riddles of Gestumblindi*. Some
of these stanzas are also in the *fornyrðislag* meter, while some are in
the related *ljóðaháttr* meter (see the Introduction to *The Wanderer's
Hávamál*, Hackett, 2019, for a discussion of this meter). It has often
been said that these are the only riddles preserved in Old Norse, but
in fact the manuscript AM 625 4to (Iceland, 1300s) has some similar
riddles about birds on its p. 77r (beginning *Bóndi nǫkkurr sendi hús-
karl sinn . . .*).

Note on Language and Spelling

The sagas translated in this volume were composed in Old Norse, the
written vernacular language of medieval Iceland and Norway. This
language, sometimes called Old West Norse, is the direct ancestor
of today's Icelandic, Norwegian, and Faroese languages and is very
closely related to Old East Norse, the ancestor of Danish and Swedish.
Old Norse is also a "first cousin" to other old Germanic languages,
such as Gothic, Old English, and Old High German, and thus dis-
tantly related (as an "aunt" or "uncle") to modern Germanic languages
such as English, German, and Dutch. Old Norse was written using
the Roman alphabet (the alphabet used for English and most other
Western European languages today) beginning in approximately AD
1150, with the addition of some new letters for sounds that the Roman
alphabet was not designed to accommodate.

In the English translations in this volume, I have rendered Old
Norse names in a less anglicized form than in my translation of the

Poetic Edda,[8] consistent with the anglicization used in my two later volumes of translations, *The Saga of the Volsungs* and *The Wanderer's Hávamál*. The names of humans and gods are written essentially as they are in standard Old Norse, with the following modifications and considerations:

1. The letter *þ* (called "thorn"), capital form *Þ*, is rendered as *th* (thus *Þórr* becomes *Thór*, and *Þórir* becomes *Thórir*). The letter *þ* represents the sound of *th* in English *worth* or *breath* or *cloth* or *thin* (not *worthy* or *breathe* or *clothe* or *then*).

2. The letter *ð* (called "eth"), capital form *Ð*, which in origin is a rounded medieval letter *d* with a crossbar, is rendered as a straight-backed, modern *d* with a crossbar, *đ* (thus *Hervard, Heidrek, Óđin, Bodvar*). This letter represents the sound of *th* in English *worthy* or *breathe* or *clothe* or *then* (not *worth* or *breath* or *cloth* or *thin*).

3. The letter *ǫ* (called "o caudata") is rendered as *o* (thus *Hervǫr* is rendered as *Hervor*). In Old Norse, the letter *ǫ* represented the sound of *o* in English *or*. This vowel has become *ö* in Modern Icelandic and usually *o* in Modern Norwegian.

4. In accordance with the usual convention of modern translators, the *-r* that ends many names in the subject (nominative) case is removed. However, the *-r* at the end of a name is left intact when it is part of the name's root and not simply a grammatical ending; the most important name of this kind is *Baldr*. By convention, the final *-r* is also left intact in names that end in *-ir*, thus *Thórir*.

I have followed the same guidelines in rendering Old Norse place-names, but I have substituted Modern Scandinavian or English-language place-names when these are available, in order to facilitate comparison with good modern maps (thus *Denmark, Lejre, Sweden*, rather than Old Norse–derived *Danmork, Hleidargard, Svíthjód*). In dealing with some well-known names for which an English rendering

---

8. In that volume, only the twenty-six letters used in English are employed, so the length of vowels is ignored, and both *þ* and *ð* are printed as *th*. Meanwhile, I rendered the Old Norse name *Óðinn* in that book as *Odin* because of its familiarity to English readers, while in later translations, consistent with the anglicization used for other names, I have written *Óđin*.

of the Old Norse word is already widespread and popular, I have used that instead of directly transliterating the Old Norse word according to the guidelines above: thus, I write *Valhalla* and *Valkyrie* instead of the more authentic or consistent *Valholl* and *Valkyrja*.

Pronunciation

The pronunciation of Old Norse in the mid-1200s AD (the early period of saga-writing in Iceland) can be reconstructed with great confidence using the tools of historical linguistics, and this reconstructed medieval pronunciation is easier to learn and more historically authentic than the Modern Icelandic pronunciation favored by many today.

In reading Old Norse aloud, keep in mind that the accent is always on the first syllable of a word, thus *ING-i-bjorg*, not *ing-i-BJORG*, and so on. The Old Norse pronunciation of most consonants is similar enough to the Modern English pronunciation to require no comment. In addition to the pronunciation of the letters unique to Old Norse (see above), the most important facts to note are these:

f is pronounced as *v*, unless at the beginning of a word; thus, the name *Hrólf* is pronounced close to what might be written in English as *HROALVE*.

g is pronounced as in *go*, never with the sound of *j* as in *gin*; thus, the second syllable of *Helgi* begins with the *g* of *geese*, not the *g* of *geode*.

j is pronounced as the English *y* in *young*, or the German *j* in *ja*; thus, *Jǫtunheimr* is pronounced *YAWT-une-hame-r*. The sequence *hj* is pronounced *hy*, as the *h* in English *Houston* or *hue*.

r is a trill, as in Scottish English or Spanish. In many words, final *-r* after another consonant constitutes its own separate syllable, not unlike the way that the final syllable in American English *water* or *bitter* is really only a syllabic *r* pronounced without a "true" vowel before it.

s is pronounced as in *bass*, never with the sound of *z* as in *has*; thus, *Áslaug* is pronounced *OSS-loug*, not *OZ-loug*.

Vowels without the acute length mark (´) are pronounced as in Spanish, so *a* is the *o* of American English *got*, *e* is the *e* of *pet*, *i* is the *ee* of *feet*, *o* is approximately the *oa* in *boat*, and *u* is the *oo* of *boot*.

The vowel *y* is similar to *u*, but farther forward in the mouth, like the German *ü* or the vowel in a "surfer" pronunciation of *dude* or *tune*. The letter *y* is not used as a consonant in Old Norse (see *j*, above). The vowel *æ* is pronounced as the *a* in *cash*, and the vowel *ø* has a pronunciation somewhat like the *i* in *bird* (more authentically, the German or Swedish *ö* or the Norwegian or Danish *ø*). A vowel with the acute length mark (´) is pronounced with the same sound as the equivalent unmarked vowel, but the syllable lasts a few fractions of a second longer (compare the words *hat* and *had* in English, where the vowel is longer in the second word than in the first). The exception is long *á*, which is pronounced with more rounding of the lips than the short vowel, similar to the *o* in many older American pronunciations of *on*, or to the *o* in a northern New Jersey pronunciation of *coffee*. The short version of the same "coffee" vowel is written *ǫ* in classical Old Norse.

The diphthong *au* is pronounced like the *ou* of *house*, while *ei* is the *ai* of *rain*. The diphthong *ey* is somewhat similar to the *oy* in *boy*, if pronounced with pursed lips (a more authentic parallel would be the Norwegian *øy*).

A Note on This Volume's Translations

The translations in this volume were prepared from the standard Old Norse texts edited by Guðni Jónsson and Bjarni Vilhjálmsson in *Fornaldarsögur Norðurlanda*, vols. 1 and 2 (Bókaútgáfan forni, 1943–44). I have generally followed the chapter divisions and divisions into "parts" and "tales" printed in that volume as well, while occasionally dividing chapters a sentence earlier or later. Decisions about punctuation (including quotation marks), capitalization, and the divisions of the Old Norse text into sentences and paragraphs are my own, and reflect natural breaks in the narrative as perceived by a reader accustomed to contemporary prose. The Old Norse text vacillates between the present and past tense in narration, but I have regularized all narration into the past tense, and I have freely translated the conjunctions between clauses and sentences to ensure an unmonotonous rhythm and style in English.

Further Reading

Crawford, Jackson (translator). *The Saga of the Volsungs, with The Saga of Ragnar Lothbrok.* Hackett, 2017.

> The two sagas in this volume are more widely known examples of the genre of mythical-heroic sagas to which both *Hrólf* and *Hervor* belong.

Crawford, Jackson (translator). *The Wanderer's* Hávamál. Hackett, 2019.

> Original Old Norse text and English translation of the Eddic poem *Hávamál*, in which the Norse god Óðin offers his practical advice for wise living. A critical monument of the early Norse culture that is reflected in *Hervor* and to a lesser extent in *Hrólf.*

Hermann Pálsson and Paul Edwards (translators). *Seven Viking Romances.* Penguin, 2005.

> The "romances" of the title are not love stories but adventures. This volume contains *The Saga of Arrow-Odd,* a long, amusing, episodic tale that includes its own very similar version of the battle on Samsø that takes places in *The Saga of Hervor and Heiðrek.*

Klaeber, Frederick, Robert E. Bjork, R. D. Fulk, and John D. Niles (editors). *Klaeber's Beowulf, Fourth Edition.* University of Toronto, 2008.

> The standard scholarly edition of *Beowulf* in Old English. Includes a vast and authoritative introduction with detailed notes on parallels with other works, such as *The Saga of Hrólf Kraki and His Champions.*

Kunz, Keneva (translator). *The Saga of the People of Laxardal and Bolli Bollason's Tale.* Penguin, 2008.

> One of the most celebrated of the "Sagas of Icelanders," more realistic sagas focused on early Icelandic settlers. King Hrólf Kraki's sword Skofnung makes an unexpected appearance here.

Ringler, Dick (translator). *Beowulf: A New Translation for Oral Delivery.* Hackett, 2007.

A remarkably well-done translation of the Old English *Beowulf*, which focuses on different members of the Skjoldung (or Scylding) royal family in early Denmark, while clearly deriving from many of the same narrative traditions that produced *The Saga of Hrólf Kraki and His Champions* in Iceland. In particular, Beowulf's arrival in Denmark and his fight with Grendel have marked similarities to Boðvar's arrival in Denmark and his fight against the monster at Hrólf's hall.

Sagas of Warrior-Poets. Various translators. Penguin, 2002.

Contains *Kormák's Saga*, another of the Sagas of Icelanders in which Hrólf Kraki's sword Skofnung reappears generations after his death.

Saxo Grammaticus (author), Karsten Friis-Jensen (editor), and Peter Fisher (translator). *Gesta Danorum (The History of the Danes), Volume I.* Clarendon Press, 2015.

A work of medieval scholarship by the Danish historian Saxo Grammaticus, who died in approximately AD 1220. Several stories in Books 2, 5, and 7 offer close analogues to the two sagas in this volume and are clearly derived from related traditions of the mythical heroes circulating in Scandinavia in Saxo's time.

Suzuki, Seiichi. *The Meters of Old Norse Eddic Poetry.* De Gruyter, 2014.

A work of profound scholarship, with a revolutionarily detailed and clear analysis of the workings of Eddic poetry (including the original poems that appear in the sagas translated in this volume).

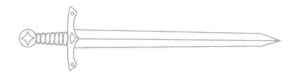

The Saga of Hervor and Heiđrek

(Hervarar saga ok Heiđreks)

Chapter 1

There was a king named Sigrlami, who ruled the Kingdom of the Rus. His daughter was Eyfura, who was the most beautiful of all women. This king had acquired a sword named Tyrfing from some dwarves, and this was the sharpest of all swords, and whenever it was drawn, it shone like a ray of sunlight. And that blade could never be unsheathed without killing a man each time, and it always had to be sheathed with warm blood on the blade. And no living thing, either human or animal, could live to see another day if it was wounded by that sword, no matter if the wound was large or small. This sword had never left a swing uncompleted or failed to cut all the way through a man to the earth beneath him, and the man who bore this sword in battle would be victorious if he fought with it. This sword is famous in all the old sagas.

A man was named Arngrím. He was an outstanding Viking. He went east into the Kingdom of the Rus and spent some time with King Sigrlami and became a leader in his army, protecting both land and men, because the king was now old. Arngrím became such a great chieftain that the king gave him his daughter in marriage, and made him the preeminent man in his kingdom. He then gave him the sword

1

Tyrfing. Then the king sat quietly at home, and nothing more is said about him.

Arngrím went with his wife Eyfura north to the lands he had inherited from his family, and they settled at the island called Bólm. They had twelve sons: the oldest and most famous was named Angantýr, the second Hjorvarð, the third Hervarð, the fourth Hrani, then the two named Hadding. No others are named. All of them were berserkers, such strong and mighty champions that they would never travel in a larger army than just the twelve of them, and yet they never entered a battle without taking the victory. Because of this they became famous throughout all lands, and there was no king who would refuse to give them whatever they wanted.

Chapter 2

It happened one Yule Eve that men were swearing oaths while drinking, as is customary, and Arngrím's sons swore oaths. Hjorvarð swore an oath that he would marry the daughter of Ingjald, King of the Swedes, a woman who was famous in all lands for her beauty and achievements, or else he would marry no woman. And in the spring the twelve brothers went together on a journey to Uppsala and went before the king's table where his daughter sat beside him.

Then Hjorvarð told the king why he had come, and the oath he had sworn, and everyone inside the hall listened. Hjorvarð asked the king to tell him quickly whether he would get what he came for or not. The king thought about this, considering what great men these brothers were and what a famous family they were from. But in that moment a man named Hjálmar the Bold stepped forward over the king's table and said, "My lord king, please recall what great honor I have won for you ever since I came to this land, and how many battles I have fought in order to subjugate lands for you. It is to you that I have given my service. Now I ask you that you reward me with honor and give me your daughter, a woman my heart has long been set on. It is more appropriate to reward me with what I ask for than to reward these berserkers, men who have done nothing but evil in your own kingdom and in many other kings' lands."

Now the king considered this twice as seriously, and he considered it a great dilemma that these two noble men were competing so vigorously for his daughter. Then the king answered in this way: "Each of these two men is so great and from such a good family," he said, that he couldn't deny his daughter to either of them, and he asked his daughter to choose which one she wanted to have.

She answered that, if it were hers to choose, and if her father really wanted her to marry, then she would choose the one who she knew was good, and not the one that she knew only from stories—and all the stories about Arngrím's sons were stories of evil.

Then Hjorvarð challenged Hjálmar to a duel south on Samsø and cursed him to be called a coward by every man if he married the woman before the duel was fought. Hjálmar said he wouldn't hesitate to fight the duel. Then the sons of Arngrím went home and told their father what had happened, and he said that never before had he feared what might happen to them.

Next the brothers went to Jarl Bjarmar, and he welcomed them with a great feast. Angantýr wanted the jarl's daughter, named Sváva, and at this feast they were married.

Then Angantýr told the jarl a dream he had had. In this dream, he and his brothers were on Samsø where they saw many wild birds, and they killed all of them. Then they turned around, and they saw two eagles coming toward them. Angantýr thought that he fought one of them, and they had a hard battle, and both he and the eagle were forced to the ground before it was over. But meanwhile the other eagle was attacking his eleven brothers, and he thought that the eagle won that battle.

The jarl said that there was no need to try to interpret this dream, and that Angantýr had foreseen the fall of powerful men.

Chapter 3

When the brothers came home, they prepared for the duel, and their father escorted them to their ship and there he gave the sword Tyrfing to Angantýr. "I think," he said, "that now there will be need for good weapons." He told them farewell, and they parted.

And when the brothers came to Samsø, they saw where two ships of the kind called *askar* were anchored in the harbor called Munarvág. They thought these ships must belong to Hjálmar and to Odd the Traveler, also known as Arrow-Odd. Then the sons of Arngrím drew their swords and bit on the ends of their shields, and the berserker fury came upon them. Six of them went out onto each ship.

There were such good warriors on these ships that they all drew their weapons, and none of them fled, and none of them spoke a downcast word. But the berserkers went from stern to prow and back again, and killed all of them. Then they went back to land howling.

Hjálmar and Odd had been on the island trying to discover whether the berserkers had arrived. Now they returned from the forest to their ships, and at this moment the berserkers came off of their ships with bloody weapons and drawn swords, and the berserker fury had left them. And this left them weaker than they were during the fury, as if they were recovering from some kind of illness. Then Odd said:

> "I feared them,
> once only,
> when they howled
> and left the ships,
> and hollered
> and came on land;
> there were twelve
> of those honorless men."

Then Hjálmar said to Odd: "You surely see that all our men are now dead, and it's likely all of us will be Óðin's guests in Valhalla tonight." Men say that these were the only words of despair Hjálmar ever said.

Odd answered, "I would advise that we flee into the forest. Two of us won't be able to take on twelve of them, who have already killed twelve of the boldest men who lived in Sweden."

Then Hjálmar said, "Let's never flee from our enemies, but instead let's face their blades. I'd rather go fight the berserkers."

Odd said, "I don't care to visit Óðin this evening, and all these berserkers ought to be dead before evening, and the two of us still alive."

This conversation of theirs is proven by these stanzas, which Hjálmar spoke:

> "Fierce men walk
> off their warships,
> twelve honorless
> men together,
> the two of us
> foster-brothers
> will visit Óðin tonight,
> and those twelve will live."

Odd said:

> "These words
> will be my answer:
> Those twelve,
> the berserkers,
> will visit Óðin tonight,
> and the two of us will live."

Hjálmar and Odd saw that Angantýr had Tyrfing in his hand, because it shone like a ray of sunlight. Hjálmar said, "Would you rather fight against Angantýr alone or against all eleven of his brothers?"

Odd said, "I'll fight Angantýr. He'll cut hard with Tyrfing, but I trust more in my shirt than in your armor as protection."

Hjálmar said, "Where did we ever fight that you went ahead of me? You want to fight with Angantýr because you think it's the greater honor. But I am the one who started this fight; I promised something else to the king's daughter in Sweden than to let you or anyone else enter into this duel for me. I will fight Angantýr." And he drew his sword and went forth against Angantýr, and they showed each other the way to Valhalla, turning against each other and leaving little space between the great swings they took at each other with their swords. Odd called out to the berserkers and said:

"One ought to fight
against one, unless
one of them is a true coward—
or his courage fails."

Then Hjorvarð came forth, and he and Odd had a hard exchange of weapon-blows. But Odd's silk shirt was so hardy that no weapon could harm it, and he had a sword so good that it bit through armor like through cloth. He took only a few swings at Hjorvarð before he fell dead. Then he went to Hervarð and it went the same way, then Hrani, then each after the other, and Odd made such a tough attack on them that he cut down all of the eleven brothers.

As to Hjálmar's duel with Angantýr, it can be told that Hjálmar sustained sixteen injuries, but not before Angantýr fell dead. Odd went to where Hjálmar was, and said:

"What's the news, Hjálmar?
Your color's changed,
and I think many wounds
are weakening you.
Your helmet's split,
your armor sags,
now I suspect
even your life has left you."

Hjálmar said:

"I have sixteen wounds,
my armor's ruined,

my sight turns black,
I can't see to walk.
Angantýr's sword
struck my heart dead—
that sharp blade,
hardened in poison."

And then he said:

"I had, at my best,
five farms altogether,
but I never loved
that way of life.
Now I must lie here
with my life gone,
wounded by a sword
on Samsø.

"Good men are
in the hall of my father,
gifted with his rings,
drinking his mead.
Drinking is what
maims many men.
As for me,
the sword's trail shows.

"I departed from
the lovely lady
on the shore
of Agnafit.
And what she told me
in that place
will be proven true,
that I'd never return.

"Take from my hand
the golden ring,
take it to the young
Ingibjorg.
It will be hard news
for her ears
that I'll never return
to Uppsala.

"I departed from
the singing of women.
With no joy or comfort,
I went east to Sóti.
I hurried that journey,
and I went in an army
for the last time,
leaving faithful friends.

"The raven flies west
off a high tree,
the eagle flies behind
in tight formation.
For the last time,
I'll give that eagle food;
that bird will get a taste
of my own blood."

After this, Hjálmar died. Odd told the news at home in Sweden, where the king's daughter could not live after Hjálmar, and killed herself. Angantýr and his brothers were laid to rest in burial mounds on Samsø with all their weapons.

Chapter 4

Bjarmar's daughter Sváva was pregnant, and gave birth to an especially beautiful girl. She was sprinkled with water and given a name, and called Hervor. She grew up with the jarl and was as strong as men are. When she came of age, she was more interested in archery and shields and swords than in weaving or tapestries. And she more often did evil than good, and when she was banned from doing this, she went into the forests and killed men for their money.

When the jarl learned about this robber, he went there with his army and captured Hervor and brought her home with him, and she then stayed at home for a while.

On one occasion, when Hervor stood outside near where some slaves were, she treated them as evilly as she usually treated everyone. But then one of the slaves said, "Hervor, you only want to do evil, and evil is all we expect from you. And that is why the jarl forbids anyone from telling you who your father was, because he thinks it would be shameful for you to know it. It was the worst slave who lay beside his daughter, and you are their child." Hervor became furious at these words, and she went before the jarl and said:

> "I don't have to
> praise our good name,
> though mother got
> Fródmar's favor.
> I thought my father
> had some courage,
> but now I'm told
> he was a pig-herder!"

The jarl said:

> "A great lie has been told
> with too little truth;
> your father was counted
> a bold man among men.

Angantýr's hall stands,
piled out of earth,
down in Samsø,
on the island's south end."

She said:

"Now I am eager,
foster-father,
to visit my departed
famous kinsmen.
They must have
owned enough riches—
I will inherit them,
unless I die first.

"First, I will quickly
take off the soft linen
from around my hair
before I depart.
It is vitally important
that tomorrow I must
have a man's shirt and cloak
tailored for me."

Afterward Hervor spoke with her mother and said:

"You wise woman,
make it all for me
as well as you can,
as you would for a son.
The truth came to me
while I slept:
I will not have joy here
for a little while."

Then she went alone, and took for herself a man's equipment and weapons. And she went to where some Vikings were, and went with them for a while and called herself Hervard. A little later this Hervard became leader of the group, and when they came to Samsø, Hervor told her men that she wanted to go out on the island, and that there was hope of treasure in the grave. But all her warriors spoke against it, telling her that there were such evil spirits walking there day and night that it was worse to be there in the daytime than it was to be out at night in other places. Soon enough, the anchor was dropped, and Hervor got into a boat and rowed to land and came to shore in Munarvág at the same time the sun was setting, and there she met a man watching a herd.

He said:

> "What kind of person
> is walking on this island?
> Be quick and go back
> to where you're staying!"

She said:

> "I will not go
> to where I'm staying,
> because I don't know
> the island's residents.
> Tell me now,
> before we part:
> Where are the graves
> of Hjorvard said to lie?"

He said:

> "Don't ask about that,
> you're not wise,
> friend of Vikings—

you've gone astray.
We ought to go as quickly
as our feet will take us—
everything in this place
is hateful to humans."

She said:

"I wouldn't care
to humor cowardice,
even if this whole island
were in flame.
Such fighters as we are,
let's not fear
any little things;
tell me what I asked!"

He said:

"Anyone would be
a fool to go farther,
especially someone going alone
into such grim darkness.
There are embers flying,
the grave mounds open,
earth and swamp burn alike—
let's run faster!"

Then he started running home to his farm, and parted from her in this way. Now the next thing Hervor saw out on the island was the grave-fire burning, and she went that way and feared nothing, though all the graves were in her path. She waded forward into these fires as though into darkness, until she came to the grave of the berserkers. Then she said:

"Wake up, Angantýr,
Hervor awakes you,
the only daughter
born to you and Sváva.
Give me from your grave
your sharp-edged blade,
the one that dwarves made
for Sigrlami.

"Hervarđ, Hjorvarđ,
Hrani, Angantýr!
I awake you all
under these tree roots,
with helmet and armor
and sharp sword,
with shield and harness
and reddened spear.

"The sons of Arngrím
are much reduced,
those cruel kinsmen
are nearly dust now;
while none of the sons
of Eyfura
will speak with me
in Munarvág.

"Hervarđ, Hjorvarđ,
Hrani, Angantýr!
May you all feel
as though your ribs
had ants between them
as you rot in your grave,
unless you give me
that sword that Dvalin made;
it doesn't befit
ghosts to bear a fine weapon."

Then Angantýr said:

> "My daughter Hervor,
> why do you call out so?
> You are only welcoming
> your own evil doom.
> You've gone insane,
> you're out of your wits,
> thinking wildly,
> when you wake up dead men.
>
> "It wasn't my father who buried me,
> nor other kinsmen;
> two men who lived
> took Tyrfing;
> but of them,
> only one lives now."

She said:

> "You don't speak true.
> May a god leave you
> to sit whole in your grave,
> if you don't have
> Tyrfing with you—
> you are reluctant
> to deliver the inheritance
> to your only child!"

Then the grave mound opened, and it was as though fire and flame were all over the grave. Then Angantýr said:

> "Hel's gate draws up,
> the grave mounds open,
> everything is in flame

on the island around.
It's an evil sight
to look out of the grave—
hurry back, young lady,
go back to your ships!"

She answered:

"You can't burn
those flames so bright at night
that the fires will
terrify me!
This woman's heart
will never tremble,
even if she sees a ghost
stand before this door."

Then Angantýr said:

"I'll tell you, Hervor,
listen to me now,
wise daughter,
hear what will happen:
Tyrfing will
destroy all
of your family, girl,
if you can believe it.

"You'll have a son,
who later
will have Tyrfing
and have faith in his strength.
Men will call
that man Heiðrek;
he will be the most powerful
under the sun's domain."

Then Hervor said:

"I seemed to be
a human woman
before I decided
to seek your hall—
now give me, from out of your grave,
the sword that hates armor,
the one dangerous to shields,
the killer of Hjálmar."

Then Angantýr said:

"Hjalmar's killer
lies beneath my shoulders,
covered completely
by flames.
I know of no woman
above the earth
who would dare
to hold that sword in hand."

Hervor said:

"I will keep
the sharp sword,
and take it in hand,
I can hold it;
I do not fear
burning flame.
And now the fire seems to flicker
as I watch it."

Then Angantýr said:

"You're a fool, Hervor,
but you have courage,
rushing upon the fire
with your eyes open.
I would happily give you
the sword from my grave,
you young girl,
I cannot deny your request."

Hervor said:

"You did well,
son of Vikings,
when you gave me
the sword from your grave.
I think it's better now,
lord, to have the sword,
than to win the whole
of Norway for my kingdom."

Angantýr said:

"You don't know it, but
you lost in this matter,
fully doomed woman.
Why do you rejoice?
Tyrfing will
destroy all
of your family, girl,
if you can believe it.

She said:

> "I will go
> to the ships,
> now this girl
> is in good spirits.
> I care little,
> friend of princes,
> how my sons
> may later clash."

He said:

> "You'll own it,
> and love it long,
> you'll keep Hjálmar's killer
> in a secret place.
> Don't touch the edges;
> there's poison on both—
> it's worse for human life
> than the cutting blade.

> "Farewell, daughter.
> I'd rather have given you
> twelve men's lives,
> power and strength,
> everything good
> that Arngrím's sons
> left behind of themselves—
> if you could believe it."

She said:

> "I'm ready to leave.
> May you all dwell

whole in the grave,
and I will hurry away.
I seem more than anything
to be between worlds,
while around me
there are fires burning."

Then she went to the ships. And when the day came, she saw that the ships were gone; the Vikings had been afraid of the noises and fires on the island. Then she found transportation away, and nothing is known about her journey before she came to Gudmund at Glasisvellir, and she stayed there at Glasisvellir through the winter, and continued to call herself Hervard.

Chapter 5

One day when Gudmund was in the middle of playing chess and had lost most of his pieces, he asked if anyone could give him some advice. Hervard went to him, and it was only a short time before Gudmund's fortunes looked better.

Then a man took up Tyrfing and drew it. Hervard saw this and took the sword from him and killed him, and then went out.

Men wanted to pursue him, but Gudmund said, "Be calm, there is not as much to avenge on that individual as you believe, because you don't know who he is. But it would cost you a good deal before you managed to take the life of that woman."

Then Hervor was out raiding for a long time and was very often victorious. And when she grew tired of this, she went home to the jarl, her mother's father. Then she went about like other young women and occupied herself with sewing and tapestries.

Hofund, Gudmund's son, learned about this, and soon he came and asked for Hervor's hand. Then he won her, and brought her home. Hofund was the wisest of men, and so prudent in settling legal disputes that he always came to the right decision, whether it concerned men of his own land or others. And from his name, the man who rules in each land and judges the matters of men is called a "hofund" [Old Norse *hǫfundr,* "chieftain/judge"].

Hofund and Hervor had two sons. The first was named Angantýr, and the other was named Heidrek. They were both big and strong men, wise and handsome. Angantýr was like his father in temperament, and wished every man well. Hofund loved him dearly, and so did all his people.

But as much good as Angantýr did, Heidrek did still more evil. Hervor loved Heidrek dearly.

Heidrek was fostered by a man named Gizur.

And one time, when Hofund hosted a feast, all the men in his kingdom were invited, except for Heidrek. Heidrek did not like this at all, and he went to the feast alone and resolved to do something evil there. And when he came into the hall, his brother Angantýr rose up to meet him and asked him to sit next to him. Heidrek was not cheerful, and sat a long time by his drink in the evening. And when his brother Angantýr went out, Heidrek talked to the two men who were sitting nearest to him, and the nature of what he said was such that they grew angry at each other, and each spoke evil to the other. Then Angantýr came back and told them to be silent. And yet another time, when Angantýr had gone out, Heidrek reminded the two men about what each one had said, and it happened that one struck the other with his fists. Then Angantýr came back and told them to settle it until the morning. But a third time, when Angantýr walked off, Heidrek asked the one who had been struck whether he had the courage to avenge himself. And he spoke until the point when this man leapt up and killed his drinking companion, and then Angantýr arrived.

When Hofund learned about what Heidrek had done, he told him to leave and not to do any more evil at this feast.

Then Heidrek and his brother Angantýr went outside into the yard and said farewell there. Then, when Heidrek had gone only a little way from the town, he decided that he had not done enough evil, and he turned back to the hall and took up a large stone and threw it at the hall, in a spot where he heard men talking in the darkness. He thought that such a stone would not have missed a man, and he went in and found a dead man and recognized him as his brother Angantýr. Heidrek then went into the hall before his father and told him this.

Hofund told him to leave and never come into his sight again, and said it would be more than fitting if he was killed or hanged.

But then Queen Hervor spoke, and said that Heidrek had done great evil, but the punishment would be terrible if he could never come again into the domain of his father, and if he must leave with no possessions to his name. But the word of Hofund held so much weight that it went as he commanded, and no one was so brave that they dared to speak for Heidrek or plead for mercy on his behalf. The queen then asked Hofund to give Heidrek some good advice at their parting. Hofund said he knew little advice to give him that the boy wouldn't follow badly.

"But because you ask, my queen, I advise him first of all that he never help any man who has killed his own lord.

"I advise him this second: That he never give freedom to a man who has murdered his comrade.

"I advise him third: Not to let his wife visit her relatives too often, even if she asks.

"And fourth: Not to stay out too late with his concubine.

"Fifth: Not to ride his best horse, if he needs to travel in a hurry.

"Sixth: That he never foster the child of a man who is higher-born than he himself is.

"But I think it's likely that he won't follow any of it."

Heidrek said his father had given this advice with ill will, and said he wouldn't feel bound by it.

Now Heidrek went outside the hall. His mother stood up and walked out with him, following him out of the yard, where she said, "Now you have done something, son, that will not allow you to come back here again, but I have a little bit of help to offer you. Here is a *mǫrk* of gold and a sword called Tyrfing that I will give you. It once belonged to Angantýr, your mother's father. No man is so unwise that he has not heard of its reputation. And if you come to a place where men exchange blows, let it be a comfort to you how often Tyrfing has been victorious in battle." Now she told him farewell, and they parted.

Chapter 6

And when Heiðrek had gone a short way, he met some men, and one of them was a captive. They asked each other the news, and Heiðrek asked what this captive man had done. They said that he had betrayed his lord. Heiðrek asked if they would take money for him, and they said yes to this. He then gave them half of the *mǫrk* of gold he had, and they let him free. The man offered Heiðrek his service, but Heiðrek said, "Why would you be true to me, an unknown man, when you betrayed your own lord? Get away from me."

A little later Heiðrek met some more men, and again one of them was a captive. He asked what this man had done wrong. They said he had murdered his comrade. He asked if they wanted money for him. They said yes to that. He gave them the other half of his *mǫrk* of gold. This man also offered Heiðrek his service, which Heiðrek declined.

Then Heiðrek wandered long roads, and finally came to a place called Reiðgotaland. The king who ruled there was named Harald. He was very old, and he had been the ruler of a large kingdom. He had no son, and his domain was shrinking because some jarls were rebelling against him with an army, and he had fought against them and never won a victory. And the king and the jarls had made peace on the condition that the king would pay them a tax every twelve months. Heiðrek stopped there in Reiðgotaland and stayed with the king during the winter.

It happened once that a great deal of money came to the king. Heiðrek asked the king whether this was the taxes paid to him by his subjects. The king said that it was the other way around: "I will pay this money in tax." Heiðrek said that it was unseemly for a king who had such a great kingdom to pay taxes to evil jarls; he said it would be a more intelligent plan to make war against them. But the king said that he had tried this and been defeated.

Heiðrek said, "I would like to repay you for your kind favor by leading an attack against them. And I would think, even if I had the choice of my troops, that it would be a small matter for me to fight alone even against nobler men than these are."

The king said, "I will give you whatever choice of troops you want, if you want to fight against the jarls, and your destiny will be good if this ends well. It is to be expected also that you will find yourself lacking, if you're exaggerating your abilities." After this the king had a large army assembled, and he prepared them for war. Heiðrek was made chieftain over this army, and he went then against these jarls, and plundered and robbed when he came into their kingdom. And when the jarls learned this, they led a great army against Heiðrek, and when they met, there was a hard battle. Heiðrek was in the forefront of the army and he had Tyrfing in his right hand, and nothing stood against that sword, neither helmet nor armor, and he dropped all the men who were nearest to him. And then he leapt forth out of the crowd and cut with both hands, and he went so far into the enemy army that he killed both jarls and afterward some of the army fled, and the greatest part was killed.

Heiðrek then went through this kingdom and placed taxes on King Harald's behalf on all the land, as there had been before, and then he went home when this was done with a great deal of money and a remarkable victory. King Harald received him with great honor and offered to let him stay and share in as much of the kingdom as he wished to ask for. Then Heiðrek asked for the hand of King Harald's daughter, who was named Helga, and she was married to him. Heiðrek then took up the rule of half of King Harald's domain. Heiðrek had a son with his wife, named Angantýr. King Harald also had a son in his old age, but he is not named.

Chapter 7

In that time there came a great famine to Reiðgotaland, and the riches of the land seemed near to disappearing. Wise men made talismans and cast lots [*blótspánn*, literally "sacrifice-woodchip" or even "sacrifice-spoon," apparently used in an unknown divination ritual], and they learned in this way that a good harvest would not come until the highest-born boy in Reiðgotaland was sacrificed. King Harald said that Heiðrek's son was the highest-born, but on the contrary Heiðrek said that it was King Harald's son who was the highest-born. And they found no way to resolve this dilemma until a journey was arranged to visit King Hofund, who could faithfully interpret all signs. Heidrek was the first man appointed for this journey, amid many other great men.

And when Heidrek came into the presence of his father, he was greeted well. He told his father his whole errand, and asked for a verdict from him. And when Hofund said that Heidrek's son was the highest-born in the land, Heidrek replied, "It seems to me that you doom my son to murder. What do you award me in compensation for the loss of my son?"

Then King Hofund said, "You must stipulate that every fourth man, out of those who are present at the place where the sacrifice is held, is to be placed into your power, or else you will not let your son be sacrificed. Then there will be no need to advise you on what you ought to do."

Now when Heidrek came home to Reidgotaland, a council was summoned. Heidrek spoke in this way: "It was the decision of King Hofund, my father, that my son is the highest-born in the land, and he is chosen for the sacrifice. But in compensation for this, I will take control of every fourth man who is present at this council, and I want you to swear this to me." And this was done, and the men gathered in his army. After this he ordered the troops summoned together and he set up a banner, and he attacked King Harald, and there came a hard battle, and King Harald fell there and much of his army. Heidrek now took to himself all the kingdom that King Harald had owned, and became king over it. Heidrek now said that he had paid for his son with all these troops who had been killed, and now he gave the slaughtered to Ódin. His wife was so furious after her father was killed that she hanged herself in the hall of the Dísir.

One summer, King Heidrek went with his army south into Hunland and fought against the king named Humli. And he won the victory and took his daughter, who was named Sifka, and brought her home with him. And the next summer he sent her home, and at this time she was with child, and later she gave birth to a boy called Hlod who was the handsomest of all men. Humli, his mother's father, fostered him.

Chapter 8

One summer, King Heidrek went with his army to Saxony. And when the Saxon king learned this, he invited him to a feast and offered to let him take what he wanted from his lands. King Heidrek accepted this. There he saw the Saxon king's daughter, lovely and beautiful to look at, and he asked for her hand and she was married to him. The festivities grew even greater, and later Heidrek went home with his wife and along with her he took a massive amount of money.

Now King Heidrek became a great warrior, and he expanded his domain in many directions. His wife often asked for permission to visit her father, and Heidrek allowed this, and her stepson Angantýr went with her.

One summer, while King Heidrek was raiding, he came to Saxony in the kingdom of his father-in-law. He left his ships in a hidden cove and went up on land with only one man with him, and at night he came to the king's town and turned toward the chamber where his wife was accustomed to sleep. Her guards were not aware of his approach. He went into the chamber and saw that a man with handsome hair slept next to her. The man who was with King Heidrek reminded Heidrek that he had taken blood vengeance for lesser injuries. Heidrek said, "I won't do that now." He took the boy Angantýr, who lay in another bed, and he cut a large lock of hair from the man who slept in the arms of his wife, and he brought both with him, the boy and the lock of hair, and then went to his ships.

In the morning, King Heidrek arrived by ship, and all the people went to greet him, and a feast was prepared. Heidrek then summoned a council, and important news was then told to him, that his son Angantýr had suddenly died. King Heidrek said, "Show me the body." The queen said that this would only increase his agony, but it was brought to him. It was a blanket, folded over itself and with a dog inside. King Heidrek said, "My son has been badly changed, if he has become a dog."

Then King Heidrek had the boy led into the council, and said that he had proof of a terrible betrayal by his queen. He revealed everything that had happened, and asked everyone to come there who could visit the council. And when almost all the people had arrived, King

Heidrek said, "The golden boy has not come." Then there was a search, and a man was found in the cook's house with a band around his head. Many then were curious why a bad slave would come to the council. And when he came, King Heidrek said, "Now you can see the one the king's daughter would rather have than me." He took the lock of hair and held it to the man's hair, and it was all of one piece. "And you, king," said Heidrek, "have been good to me, and thus your kingdom will have peace from me, but I don't want your daughter anymore." Now Heidrek went home to his kingdom with his son.

One summer, King Heidrek sent men to the Rus to offer to bring the Rus king's son home for Heidrek to foster, because Heidrek now wanted to try to break all of his father's good advice. The messengers met with the Rus king and told him their errand and message of friendship. The Rus king answered that there was little hope that he'd place his son in the hands of a man who was known for many evil deeds. Then the queen said, "Don't say that, my lord; you have heard how important a man he is and how favored by victory, and it is a greater wisdom to accept his honor well, as otherwise your kingdom will not be at peace."

The king said, "You're working hard for this." So the boy was given into the hands of the messengers, and they went home. King Heidrek greeted the boy well and gave him a good upbringing, and loved him very much. Sifka, daughter of Humla, was there for a second time with the king, but Heidrek was warned that he ought not to tell Sifka anything that was best hidden.

Chapter 9

One summer the Rus king sent Heidrek an invitation to come east to receive a feast and a declaration of friendship from him. Heidrek got prepared with a great many men accompanying him, and the king's son and Sifka went with him. Then Heidrek went east into the Rus kingdoms and received a spectacular feast there. One day during this feast the kings went into the forest, together with a great army, to hunt with dogs and hawks. And when they let the dogs loose, each of the kings went his own way through the forest.

King Heiđrek's foster-son went with him. Heiđrek said to him, "Listen to my command, foster-son. The town is not far from here; go there and hide yourself, and take this ring as payment. Then be ready to come home, when I order them to search for you."

The boy said he was not eager for this journey, but he did as the king asked nonetheless. Heiđrek acted uncheerful when he came home that evening, and he sat only a short while at the drinking. And when he went to bed, Sifka said, "Why are you so uncheerful, lord? What is wrong with you? Are you sick? Tell me."

King Heiđrek said, "It is difficult for me to tell you, because my life is on the line if it is not kept secret."

She said she would keep it secret and she became gentle with him and acted lovingly. Then he told her, "The king's son and I were standing by a certain tree. Then my foster-son asked for an apple that was high up in the tree. Then I drew Tyrfing, and I cut down the apple, and it was done before I realized what this meant, because Tyrfing must always cause a man's death if it is drawn, and the two of us were the only ones there. So I killed the boy."

The next day the Rus queen asked Sifka why Heiđrek was so uncheerful. She said, "There is enough reason—he killed your son," and then she told the whole story.

The queen said, "This is important news, and we ought not to let it come to public attention." Then the queen went straight out of the hall in great agony of spirit.

The king discovered this and called Sifka to him and said, "What did you and the queen talk about that affected her so much?"

"My lord," she said, "a terrible thing has happened. Heiđrek has killed your son, and I suspect it was done willingly, and he deserves death."

The Rus king ordered Heiđrek taken and chained, "And it has now happened as I guessed it would." But King Heiđrek had become so popular that no one wanted to do this. Then two men stood in the hall and said no one ought to hesitate, and they put chains on him. These were both men Heiđrek had freed from death.

Then Heidrek sent men in secret for the king's son, while the Rus king ordered his people to gather together and told them that he would have Heidrek hanged on the gallows.

And at that moment the king's son came running to his father and told him not to do such a shameful deed as to kill the finest of men and his own foster-father.

Heidrek was now freed, and he prepared immediately to depart for home. Then the queen said, "My lord, don't let Heidrek go away in such a manner, with you two not at peace. That does not benefit your kingdom. Instead, offer him gold and silver." The king did so, ordering a great amount of money brought to King Heidrek, and he said he wanted to give him friendship and have his friendship still.

Heidrek said, "I don't lack money."

The Rus king told his wife this, and then she said, "Then offer him a kingdom and great possessions, and men to follow him." The king did so.

King Heidrek said, "I have enough possessions and men."

The Rus king told his wife this, and she said, "Then offer him what he wants, and that is your daughter."

Then the Rus king went to meet King Heidrek and he said, "Rather than part with hostility between us, I want you to take my daughter as your wife with as much honor as you yourself choose." King Heidrek now received this cheerfully, and the daughter of the Rus king went home with him.

Now King Heidrek had come home, and he wanted to move Sifka out. [They went riding together.] They took his best horse, and it was late in the evening. They came to a river. Now she leaned forward into him, so that the horse collapsed, and the king dismounted. Then he had to carry her over the river. There was no other solution except for him to drop her off his shoulders and break her spine asunder, and in this way he parted from her, and the river drowned her.

King Heidrek then ordered a great feast prepared, and there he married the daughter of the Rus king; their daughter was named Hervor. She was a shieldmaiden and grew up in England with Jarl Fródmar. King Heidrek now reigned in peace and became a great chieftain and a noted wise man.

King Heiðrek had a large boar brought up, as big as the biggest old bulls, and so handsome that every hair seemed to be made of gold. The king laid a hand on the head of the boar, and twelve others on his whiskers, and swore that no man had ever done so badly to him that he would not have a proper trial by his wisdom, and those twelve men were assigned to watch the boar. But a man could otherwise win a trial by bringing riddles to Heiðrek that he could not guess. King Heiðrek now became the most popular of kings.

Chapter 10

There was a man named Gestumblindi, a powerful man and a mighty enemy of King Heiðrek. The king sent him a summons to come to his court, commanding him to reconcile with him if he wanted to live. Gestumblindi was no wise man, and he knew that he was ill-prepared to exchange words with the king, and also that he could not be sure to win his case in the court of his wisdom, because his crimes were so great. So Gestumblindi sacrificed to Óðin and asked the god to represent him in court, and prayed to him to look upon his situation, and pledged to him great riches.

One night very late there was a knock at the door, and Gestumblindi went to the door and saw that a man had come. He asked the man his name and he said it was Gestumblindi, and he said that they ought to exchange clothes. They did so. The farmer Gestumblindi now went and hid himself, and the visitor came in, and everyone thought that they recognized him as Gestumblindi, and the night passed.

On the day after, this Gestumblindi made his visit to meet the king, and he greeted the king well. The king was silent. "My lord," he said, "I came here because I want to be reconciled with you."

Then the king said, "Will you suffer the judgment of my wisdom?"

Gestumblindi said, "Are there no other options?"

The king said, "There are other options, if you think you're capable of posing some riddles."

Gestumblindi said, "I feel little able to do that, though the other way seems hard."

"Would you," asked the king, "rather endure the judgment of my wisdom?"

"I choose," said Gestumblindi, "to pose riddles to you."

"That is right, and well in accordance with the law," said the king. Then Gestumblindi said:

"I wish I had
what I had yesterday,
you know what it was:
the squeezer-out of songs,
the stopper of words,
and the caster-out of words.
King Heidrek,
consider the riddle!"

The king said, "Your riddle is good, Gestumblindi, and I've guessed it. Bring him beer! It lames the wisdom of many, and many are made wordier when they get a little beer, and for some it weighs down the tongue so that they will not speak a word."
Then Gestumblindi said:

"I left my home,
I made a journey from home,
and I saw a road of roads.
There was a road under it,
and a road over it,
and a road on every side.
King Heidrek,
consider the riddle!"

"Your riddle is good, Gestumblindi, and I've guessed it. You walked on a bridge over a river, and the river was a road under you, and birds flew over your head and past you on both sides, and those were their roads."
Then Gestumblindi said:

"What's the drink
that I drank yesterday?

It wasn't wine or water,
nor was it beer,
and it wasn't any sort of food,
yet I went thirst-less after?
King Heiðrek,
consider the riddle!"

"Your riddle is good, Gestumblindi, and I've guessed it. You rested in the shade, where there was dew on the grass, and you cooled your lips with it and thus quenched your thirst."
Then Gestumblindi said:

"What's that loud thing
that walks hard roads
that he's already gone over?
He has a strong kiss,
this one with two mouths—
and he walks on gold alone.
King Heiðrek,
consider the riddle!"

"Your riddle is good, Gestumblindi, and I've guessed it. That's a hammer owned by a goldsmith. It makes a loud sound, when it hits a hard place, and that is its road."
Then Gestumblindi said:

"What kind of wonder
did I see outside,
before Delling's doors?
Two, who were not alive,
and hardly even breathing,
were cooking a sword.
King Heiðrek,
consider the riddle!"

"Your riddle is good, Gestumblindi, and I have guessed it. That was a smith's bellows. They have no wind, but they are blown, and they are dead like other tools, but with them one could make a sword or other things."

Then Gestumblindi said:

"What kind of wonder
did I see outside,
before Delling's doors?
It had eight feet,
but four eyes,
and knees higher than its belly.
King Heidrek,
consider the riddle!"

"That is a spider."

Then Gestumblindi said:

"What kind of wonder
did I see outside,
before Delling's doors?
It had its head
pointing Hel-ward,
but its feet turned to the sun.
King Heidrek,
consider the riddle!"

"Your riddle is good, Gestumblindi, and I've guessed it. That's an onion. Its head is planted in the earth, but it branches out as it grows up."

Then Gestumblindi said:

"What kind of wonder
did I see outside,
before Delling's doors?

It was harder than horn,
blacker than a raven,
whiter than a shield,
and straighter than a spear.
King Heiðrek,
consider the riddle!"

Heiðrek said, "Your riddles are getting worse, Gestumblindi. Why would I need to sit over this one long? It's obsidian, and a sun-ray shines on it."
Then Gestumblindi said,

"Very blonde brides,
two serving-women,
brought ale to a room.
It wasn't molded by hands,
nor forged by a hammer,
yet the one that made it
sat upright outside,
by some islands.
King Heiðrek,
consider the riddle!"

"Your riddle is good, Gestumblindi, and I've guessed it. Those were swan-brides who went to their nest and laid eggs. The shell of the egg is not molded by hands nor forged by a hammer. And a male swan, who fathered their eggs, sat upright outside by some islands."
Then Gestumblindi said:

"Who are these ugly women
on a remote mountain:
a wife has a child by a woman,
and that one has a son,
and those wives have no husbands?
King Heiðrek,
consider the riddle!"

"Your riddle is good, Gestumblindi, and I've guessed it. Those are two celery plants, and there's a shoot of a new one between them."
Then Gestumblindi said:

"I saw an earth-dweller
from the soil,
a worm sat on a corpse.
A blind one rode a blind one
to the wave-filled sea,
on a horse without breath.
King Heidrek,
consider the riddle!"

"Your riddle is good, Gestumblindi, and I've guessed it. There you found a dead horse on an ice floe, and a dead worm on the horse, and all of it was being carried along in the current of a river."
Then Gestumblindi said:

"Who are those men
who ride to the assembly
together, all at peace,
sent by their leader
over other lands
to build a residence?
King Heidrek,
consider the riddle!"

"Your riddle is good, Gestumblindi, and I've guessed it. That's Ítrek and Andad, when they sit playing board games."
Then Gestumblindi said:

"Who are those brides
who surround their lord,
a man who is weaponless?
The brunettes defend

all their days,
and the blondes travel.
King Heiðrek,
consider the riddle!"

"Your riddle is good, Gestumblindi, and I've guessed it. That's the
board game *hnefatafl*; the darker pieces defend the king piece, and the
white pieces attack it."
Then Gestumblindi said:

"Who is that one
who sleeps in the ashes,
and arises from stone?
Eager to be handsome,
he has no father nor mother
when he is born.
King Heiðrek,
consider the riddle!"

"That is fire hidden in a hearth, and it is lit from a flint."
Then Gestumblindi said:

"Who is that great one
who passes over the earth,
swallowing wood and water?
He fears wind,
but never men,
and sings blame at the sun.
King Heiðrek,
consider the riddle!"

"Your riddle is good, Gestumblindi, and I've guessed it. It is fog; it
passes over the earth so that nothing can be seen through it, not even
the sun. But it disappears when a wind strikes it."

Then Gestumblindi said:

> "What kind of animal
> kills men's cattle [or money]
> and has an iron shell?
> It has eight horns [or corners],
> but no head,
> and many follow it.
> King Heiðrek,
> consider the riddle!"

"That is the the *húnn*-piece in the *hnefatafl* game." [This riddle relies on some homonyms in Old Norse: *húnn* is a bear cub, but also a playing piece in the *hnefatafl* game. The identical words for "horn" and "corner" in Old Norse (both *horn*) also give the playful sense that a dangerous animal is being talked about rather than a game piece.]

The Gestumblindi said:

> "What kind of animal
> protects Danes,
> has a bloody back,
> and saves men,
> meets spears,
> gives life to some,
> and lays its body
> against a man's palm?"

"That is a shield. It is often bloody in battles, and it protects men well if they are skilled with it."

Then Gestumblindi said:

> "Who are those girls
> who pass over lands
> to spy for their father?
> They keep a white shield

in the wintertime,
but a black one in summer?"

"Those are ptarmigans; they're white in winter, but black in summer."
Then Gestumblindi said:

"Who are those girls
who walk, sorrowing,
to spy for their father?
They have done injury
to many men,
and that's how they live.
King Heidrek,
consider the riddle!"

"Those are the daughters of Ægir, the waves, that's what they're called."
Then Gestumblindi said:

"Who are those girls
who walk, in a large group,
to spy for their father?
They have blonde hair,
the white-clothed girls,
and those wives have no husbands."

"Those are waves, that's what they're called."
Then Gestumblindi said:

"Who are those widows
who walk, in a large group,
to spy for their father?
They're seldom cheerful
when they meet people,

and they must wake in the wind.
King Heiđrek,
consider the riddle!"

"Those are Ægir's widows, that's what waves are called."
Then Gestumblindi said:

"A certain goose
was once quite large;
she wanted children,
and built a home.
Hay-destroyers
defended her,
and a drink's wilderness
loomed over her."

"There a duck built her nest between a cow's jawbones, and the
skull lay over her."
Then Gestumblindi said:

"Who is the great one
who rules many,
and is halfway turned to Hel?
It protects men
and seeks earth,
if he has a trusted friend.
King Heiđrek,
consider the riddle!"

"Your riddle is good, Gestumblindi, and I've guessed it. That's an
anchor with a good rope. If it's in the seafloor, then it protects."
Then Gestumblindi said:

"Who are those brides
who walk in seaside skerries

and journey along a fjord?
Those white-clothed women
have a hard bed,
and they play little in good weather."

"Those are waves, and their beds are skerries and stones, and they
are not often visible in good weather."
Then Gestumblindi said:

"In the summer, I saw
very unhappy people,
around sunset—
I said good-bye.
Silent jarls
drank ale,
but the ale-keg
stood screaming.
King Heiðrek,
consider the riddle!"

"There you saw piglets drinking from a sow, and she squealed in
reaction."
Then Gestumblindi said:

"What kind of wonder
did I see outside,
before Delling's doors?
It had ten tongues,
twenty eyes,
forty feet—
and that creature walked.
King Heiðrek,
consider the riddle!"

The king said then, "If you are Gestumblindi, like I thought, then you are wiser than I anticipated. Now you're talking about the sow out in the yard."

Then the king ordered the sow killed, and it had nine piglets [inside it], like Gestumblindi said. Now the king suspected who this man must be. Then Gestumblindi said:

> "Four hang,
> four walk,
> two show the way,
> two fight off the dogs,
> one droops behind
> and is always dirty.
> King Heidrek,
> consider the riddle!"

"Your riddle is good, Gestumblindi, and I've guessed it. That's a cow."

Then Gestumblindi said:

> "I sat on a sail,
> I saw dead men
> holding bloody flesh
> in bark from a tree."

"There you sat on a wall [*veggr*, also meaning "sail"] and watched a falcon [*valr*, also meaning "men dead in battle"] take a duck to the cliffs."

Then Gestumblindi said:

> "Who are the two
> who have ten feet,
> three eyes,
> and one tail?
> King Heidrek,
> consider the riddle!"

"That is when Óđin rides Sleipnir."

Then Gestumblindi said:

> "Tell me this last,
> if you are wiser than every king:
> What did Óđin say
> in Baldr's ear,
> before he put him on the funeral pyre?"

King Heiđrek said, "Only you know that, you vile creature." And then Heiđrek drew Tyrfing and struck at him, but Óđin turned into a falcon and flew away. But when the king struck a second time he cut off his tail-feathers, and this is why the falcon has been so short-tailed ever since.

Then Óđin said, "For this, King Heiđrek, that you drew a weapon on me, and wished to kill me without cause, you will be killed by the worst slaves." And after this, they parted ways.

Chapter 11

It is said that King Heiđrek had some slaves, captured by him when he raided in the west. There were nine of them altogether, men of high families who thought poorly of being slaves. And it was on one night when King Heiđrek lay in his bedroom with few men near him that the slaves took weapons for themselves and went before the king's door and killed first the guards on the outside. Then they went to the king's door with fierce energy, and broke it, and killed King Heiđrek and all the others who were inside. They took the sword Tyrfing and all the treasure that was within, and they went away.

At first no one knew who had done this or where vengeance could be sought. Then Angantýr, son of King Heiđrek, summoned a council, and at this council he was taken for king over all the domains that King Heiđrek had ruled. At this council he swore an oath that he would never sit in his father's throne before he had avenged him.

A short time after this, Angantýr disappeared on his own and searched widely for these men. One evening he came to a lake while following the river that is called the Graf River. There he saw three men on a fishing boat, and in short order one of the men caught a fish and called to another, asking him to get him the fishing knife so that he could cut its head off. But this one said the knife couldn't be loaned out right then. So the first said, "Take the sword from under the headboard and get that for me," and took it from the other and drew it and cut the head from the fish, and then he said:

"By the mouth of the Graf,
a pikefish has paid
for when Heidrek was killed
under the Carpathian range."

Angantýr immediately recognized Tyrfing. Then he went away into the forest and waited there until darkness fell. And the fishermen rowed to land and went to their tent and lay down to sleep. Near midnight, Angantýr came to the tent and struck through it and killed all the nine slaves, and took the sword Tyrfing, which was a proof that he had avenged his father. Angantýr now went home.

Soon thereafter Angantýr had a great feast on the Dnieper at the settlement that is called Árheimar, to honor his father. At this time these kings ruled the lands, as it is told:

They say Humli
once ruled the Huns,
Gizur the Geats,
Angantýr the Goths,
Valdar the Danes,
Kjár the Foreigners,
and Alrek the Bold
ruled the English tribe.

Hloð, son of King Heidrek, grew up with King Humli, his mother's father, and he was the handsomest of all men and the most courageous.

And it was a saying of this time that a man was born either with weapons or horses. And what lay behind this was that either weapons were made at about the same time as the man was born, or on the other hand some kind of cattle, animals, steers, or horses were born at the same time as he was. And such things as these were all brought together to honor high-born men, as here it is said about Hloð, son of Heiðrek:

> Then Hloð was born
> in Hunland,
> with a knife and a sword,
> a long chainmail coat,
> a ring-decorated helmet,
> a sharp sword,
> and a well-tamed horse
> in the holy woods.

Now Hloð learned of the death of his father Heiðrek, and along with it that Angantýr, his brother, had been taken for king over the whole domain that their father had ruled. Now King Humli and Hloð wished that Hloð might go to Angantýr to ask for his share of the inheritance, first by means of kind words, as it says here:

> Hloð, heir of Heiðrek,
> rode from the east,
> he came to the enclosure
> where the Goths dwelled,
> in Árheimar,
> to demand his inheritance.
> There Angantýr toasted
> the fallen Heiðrek.

Now Hloð came into Árheimar with a great army, as it says here:

> Hloð found a man outside,
> in front of that high hall,

> late in the evening,
> and he said:
> "Go inside, man,
> into that high hall,
> tell Angantýr
> we need to speak!"

The messenger went in before the king's table and greeted King Angantýr well and then said this:

> "Hlod the Warlike,
> Heidrek's heir,
> your brother,
> has come here.
> That big young man
> is on horseback,
> and he wants to speak
> with you, my lord."

And when the king heard this, he threw his knife onto the table, and then flung the table over and threw his armor on and took his white shield in hand, and the sword Tyrfing in his other hand. Then there arose a great noise in the hall, as it says here:

> There was a noise in the house,
> the nobles stood up,
> each wanted to hear
> what Hlod would say
> and what Angantýr
> would answer.

Then Angantýr said, "Welcome, Hlod my brother, come in and drink with us, and let us drink mead together first in honor of our father, and then to dignify all of us in our pride."

Hloð said, "I have come for a different reason than to get a drink in my belly." Then he said:

"I want half of everything
that Heiðrek owned:
half the cows, half the calves,
half the whistling millstones,
half the needles, half the spears,
half the treasure,
half the slaves, men and women,
and half their children.

"Half the great forest
called Mirkwood,
half the holy graves
in the Goths' lands,
half the lovely stone
which stands by the Dnieper,
half the armor
Heiðrek owned,
half the lands and men
and bright rings."

Then Angantýr said, "You have not come lawfully to this land, and you want to make a crooked offer." Then Angantýr continued,

"Brother, first
the white shield must break,
and the cold spear
meet another of its kind,
and many a man
kneel dead in the grass,
before I split Tyrfing
in two pieces,
before I give you, son of a Hun,
half the inheritance!"

And Angantýr said further,

> "I will offer you
> bright spears, money,
> a heaping portion of the wealth
> that will please you most;
> twelve hundred men,
> twelve hundred horses,
> twelve hundred servants
> who each bear a shield.

> "I will give each man
> many other things,
> better than he
> has a right to have.
> I'll give each man
> a young bride,
> I'll put a necklace
> on every bride's neck.

> "I will measure out
> silver for you while you sit,
> and weigh you down
> with gold while you stand,
> so rings roll off you
> in every direction,
> and you will have the rule
> of a third of the Goths."

Chapter 12

Gizur of the Grýtings, foster-father of Angantýr, was with King Angantýr then, and he was very old. And when he heard Angantýr's offer, he thought too much was being given away, and he said:

"All this, to be received
by a slavewoman's son?
He's a slavewoman's son,
even if fathered by a king!
A bastard son
sat on a grave mound
when a noble-born son
shared out his inheritance."

Hloð became extremely angry that he would be called a slavewoman's son and a bastard, if he accepted his brother's offer, and so he left immediately with all his men, going all the way to Hunland, to King Humli his kinsman. He told him that Angantýr his brother had not granted him a half share in the inheritance. Humli then learned all of what they had said, and he became extremely angry that his grandson Hloð was called a serving-woman's son, and he said then:

"We'll remain here this winter,
and live happily,
we'll judge, and we'll drink
from precious cups.
We'll teach the Huns
to hold their war-weapons,
weapons we'll later lead them
boldly into battle holding."

And then he said:

"Hloð, we'll prepare
an army for you well,
and we'll bravely
make war,
the Huns will summon
an army, composed
of twelve-year-old boys,
and two-year-old foals."

During this winter, Humli and Hlod sat quietly. During the spring, they assembled such a huge army that there was nothing left over of the fighting-age men of Hunland. All men twelve years old and older came, if they were able to fight with weapons, together with all the horses two years old or older. It was such a great gathering of men that it would have to be counted in the thousands, and in nothing less than thousands. And a chieftain was placed over each regiment, and a banner over each regiment, and there were 15,600 in each regiment, and each regiment had thirteen battalions, and in each battalion there were 160 men, and there were thirty-three such regiments. And when this army came together, they rode through the forest called Mirkwood that separates Hunland from the lands of the Goths. And as they emerged from the forest, there were large settlements and flat plains, and on the valley stood a fair city. And there Hervor, sister of King Angantýr, ruled, together with Ormar, her foster-father. They had been placed there in order to guard the land from the army of the Huns, and they had many troops there.

Chapter 13

It was one morning at sunrise that Hervor stood high on a certain castle over the city wall, and she saw a great cloud of dust kicked up by horses south toward the forest, so large that it hid the sun for a long while. Then she saw, glowing under the dust cloud as if she were looking at a piece of gold jewelry, beautiful shields inlaid with gold, gilded helmets, and bright coats of chainmail. Then she saw that it was the army of the Huns, and they were very numerous. Hervor went down quickly and called to a trumpeter, telling him to sound the alarm. And then Hervor said, "Take your weapons and get ready for battle! And you, Ormar, ride toward the Huns and offer them a battle below the southern wall of the city." And Ormar said:

"I will certainly ride
holding the shield,

and offer war on behalf
of the army of Goths."

Then Ormar rode from the city toward the army. He called out loudly and told them to ride to the city, "and out below the southern wall of the city, that's where I offer you battle. Let those who come first wait for the others' arrival."

Now Ormar rode back to the city, and Hervor was now prepared as was the whole army. They now rode out of the city toward the Huns, and a terrible battle began. But because the Huns had the much bigger army, the bulk of the casualties were in Hervor's army, and in time she fell and much of her army fell around her. And when Ormar saw her fall, he fled, as did all the other survivors. Ormar rode day and night, as hard as he could, until he came to King Angantýr in Árheimar.

Now the Huns began to raid the whole land and burn it. And when Ormar came to King Angantýr, he said:

> "I've come from the south
> to tell you this,
> the famous forest of Mirkwood
> is all burned to cinders,
> and all the Gothic warriors
> are covered in men's blood.

> "I know that Hervor,
> Heiðrek's daughter,
> your sister,
> was bent to the earth,
> it's the Huns
> who have felled her,
> and many others
> of your warriors.

> "She found it easier to go to war
> than to speak to suitors,
> or to sit and drink
> on her wedding day."

King Angantýr grinned when he heard this. He paused a long time before speaking, and then he said:

> "You were treated unbrotherly,
> you excellent sister."

And then he looked over his shoulder, and there were not many troops with him. He said:

> "There were many of us
> when we drank mead,
> and now we are fewer
> when we ought to be more.

> "I don't see a single man
> in my army
> who would ride
> and bear the shield,
> and seek out the fighters
> of the Huns
> (although I might ask,
> and I might pay him with rings)."

Gizur the Old said:

> "I will ask you
> for not one coin,
> not one jingling
> piece of gold.
> But I will ride
> and bear the shield,
> and offer war
> to the Hunnish troops."

It was a law of King Heiđrek, that if an army was in the land and the enemy king staked out a valley and chose a battlefield, then the invaders could not raid until they had a battle. Gizur armed himself with good weapons and leapt onto his horse like a young man. Then he said to the king:

> "Where shall I show
> the Huns our battlefield?"

Angantýr said:

> "You remember
> the slaughter
> at Dúnheiđ, under the
> Jassar Mountains.
> There the Goths
> have often made war
> and famously
> won victory."

Now Gizur rode away until he came to the Hunnish army. He did not ride any nearer than he needed to be heard by them. Then he called out in a high voice and said:

> "Your army is frightened!
> Your king is doomed!
> Battle-flags overshadow you,
> Óđin will be fierce to you."

And then:

> "I offer you
> a slaughter at Dúnheiđ,
> a battle, under the
> Jassar Mountains.

You'll each be raw flesh
in those high places!
Now may Óðin let the spear fly
in accord with what I say!"

When Hloð had heard the words of Gizur, he said:

"Capture Gizur
of the Grýting people,
that man of Angantýr
who's come from Árheimar!"

King Humli said:

"We won't do harm
to messengers,
those who travel
all alone."

Gizur said, "The Huns will not make us afraid, nor will your bows
made of horn." Then he spurred his horse and rode to King Angantýr
and went before him and he greeted him well. The king asked whether
he had met the kings. Gizur said, "I spoke with them, and I summoned them to a battlefield at Dúnheið in the valleys of slaughter."
Angantýr asked how large an army the Huns had. Gizur said, "Their
numbers are great,

"There are six
regiments of men,
and in each regiment
five battalions;
in each battalion
thirteen squadrons;
in each squadron
the men are quadrupled."

Angantýr now knew about the Hunnish army, and so he sent his men away in every direction, summoning every man to come who would help his army and knew how to use weapons. Then he went to Dúnheid with his army, and that was an incredibly large army. And then the Huns came against them, and they had an army half again as large.

Chapter 14

On the second day, they began their battle, and they fought all day, and in the evening they went into their tents. They fought in this way for eight days, and the chieftains remained uninjured, though no one knew the count of how many men fell.

By both day and night, new troops arrived for Angantýr from every direction, and thus it came to be that he had no fewer men than he had at first. And the battle grew yet fiercer all the time. All of the Huns were thoroughly vicious, and they now understood the stakes, which did not include keeping their lives if they did not win the battle. They knew there would be no point in begging the Goths for mercy.

For their part, the Goths guarded their freedom and their homeland from the Huns, and they stood firm and encouraged one another. And when the day had advanced, the Goths attacked so hard that the troops of the Huns bent like stalks of grass before them. And when Angantýr saw this, he came forward from his shield-wall and entered the front of the fighting force and had Tyrfing in his hand, and he swung it at both men and horses. The shield-wall of the Kings of the Huns broke then, and Angantýr exchanged blows with his brother Hlod. Then Hlod fell, and King Humli, and then the Huns broke out into retreat, but the Goths killed them and felled so many men that the rivers were dammed up and overflooded their banks, and the valleys were full of dead horses and men and blood. Then King Angantýr went to inspect the fallen, and he found Hlod, his brother. Then he said:

> "Brother, I offered you
> an undiminished inheritance—

money, and a horde of jewels—
which befit you as a king.
Now you have neither
bright rings, nor even
your lands, at the end,
as the wages of your battle."

And then:

"We two are cursed, brother,
and I have become your killer.
This will be remembered forever,
and the judgment of the Norns is evil."

Chapter 15

Angantýr was king of Reiðgotaland a long time. He was a powerful
and great warrior, and many families of kings are descended from
him. His son was Heiðrek Wolf-skin, who afterward was king for
a long time in Reiðgotaland. He had a daughter named Hild, who
was mother of Hálfdan the Clever, who was the father of Ívar the
Wide-conquering. Ívar the Wide-conquering came to Sweden with an
army, as it says in the sagas of kings, and King Ingjald the Evil-advised
feared his army and burned himself in his home with all his guards
at the settlement called Ræning. Ívar the Wide-conquering then took
all Sweden as his domain, and he also conquered the Danish kingdom
and the Baltic shore, as well as Saxony and Estonia and all the east as
far as the Rus kingdom. And he ruled West Saxony and won a part of
England called Northumberland. Ívar placed all of the Danish kingdom under his control and then made Valdar king over it, and gave
him his daughter Álfhild as wife. Their sons were Harald War-tooth
and Randvér, who fell in England. Valdar later died in Denmark,
when Randvér took Denmark as his own and became king over it.
But Harald War-tooth took the title of king in Götaland, and later

he brought under himself all the kingdoms earlier mentioned, those that King Ívar the Wide-conquering had owned. King Randvér was married to Ása, daughter of King Harald the Red-whiskered from the north in Norway. Their son was Sigurd Ring. King Randvér died suddenly, and Sigurd Ring took the kingdom in Denmark. He fought with King Harald War-tooth at Brávellir in eastern Götaland, and there King Harald fell and much of his army with him. These battles have been the most famous in old sagas, and they were the scenes of the greatest loss of life, together with the battle that Angantýr and his brother fought at Dúnheid. King Sigurd Ring ruled the Danish kingdom until his dying day, and his son Ragnar Lodbrók ruled after him.

The son of Harald War-tooth was named Eystein the Evil-advised. He took Sweden after his father and ruled it until the sons of King Ragnar killed him, as it says in his saga. The sons of King Ragnar then took over the rule of Sweden, and after the death of King Ragnar, his son Bjorn Ironside took over the rule of Sweden, and Sigurd took the Danish kingdom, and Hvítserk the east, and Ívar the Boneless took England.

The sons of Bjorn Ironside were Eirík and Refil. Bjorn was a warking and a sea-king, and King Eirík ruled Sweden after his father and lived only a short time. Then Eirík, son of Refil, took the kingdom. He was a great warrior and a very mighty king. The sons of Eirík, son of Bjorn Ironside, were Onund from Uppsala and King Bjorn. Then Sweden came once again to be divided among the brothers when they took over the kingdom from Eirík Refilsson. King Bjorn took the settlement called Haug, and he was called Bjorn at Haug. Bragi the poet was with him. Eirík was the son of King Onund who took over the kingdom at Uppsala after his father. He was a mighty king.

In his time, Harald Fair-hair came to the throne in Norway, the first man of his family who ruled Norway as one kingdom. Bjorn was a son of King Eirik in Uppsala. He took over the reign of the kingdom after his father and ruled a long time. The sons of Bjorn were Eirík the Victorious and Óláf; they took the dominion and the kingdom after their father. Óláf was the father of Styrbjorn the Strong. In their time, King Harald Fair-hair died.

Styrbjorn fought with King Eirík, his father's brother, at Fýrisvellir, and Styrbjorn died there. Then Eirík ruled Sweden until his death-day.

He was married to Sigríð Great-advisor. Their son was named Óláf, who was taken as king in Sweden after King Eirík. He was a child then, and the Swedes carried him after themselves, and for this reason he was called Óláf Tax-king, and later Óláf the Swede. He was a mighty king for a long time. He was the first of the Swedish kings to accept Christianity, and during his rule Sweden was called Christian. Onund was the name of the son of King Óláf the Swede, who ruled after him and died of sickness. In his time, King Óláf the Holy [of Norway] died at Stiklastad. Eymund was the name of the second son of Óláf the Swede, who ruled after his brother. In his time, the Swedes were not good Christians. Eymund was king for a short time.

Chapter 16

Steinkel was the name of a powerful man of noble birth in Sweden. His mother was Ástríð, the daughter of Njál Finnsson the Squinter from Hálogaland [in Norway], and his father was Rognvald the Old. Steinkel was the highest jarl in Sweden, and after the death of King Eymund the Swedes took him as their king. It was thus that, at this time, the rule of Sweden passed out of the hands of the descendants of the ancient kings.

Steinkel was a great chieftain. He married a daughter of King Eymund. He died of sickness in Sweden around the same time as King Harald [Hard-ruler, of Norway] died in England. Ingi was the name of a son of Steinkel who became king of the Swedes after Hákon. Ingi was king there for a long time, and he was popular and a good Christian. He ended the practice of sacrifices in Sweden and told all the people to convert to Christianity, but the Swedes had too much false belief in the heathen gods and held on to their ancient rituals. King Ingi wanted to marry a woman named Mey [Girl], whose brother was named Svein [Boy]. King Ingi liked no man as much as he did Svein, and he became the most powerful man in Sweden. But the Swedes thought King Ingi broke the old laws of the land when he opposed the practices that Steinkel had allowed to continue. At a certain meeting that the Swedes had with King Ingi, they gave him two choices: either to hold the old laws or to give up the kingship. Then King Ingi said he would not cast off the faith that was right. Then the Swedes screamed and they pelted him with stones and drove him away from the meeting grounds. Svein, the brother-in-law of the king, remained behind at the meeting. He offered to make a sacrifice on the Swedes' behalf, if they would give him the kingship. They all agreed to that, and Svein was taken as king over all of Sweden. Then a horse was brought to the meeting and cut apart. They ate it, and smeared the sacrifice-tree with its blood. They forsook Christ, made sacrifices, and drove Ingi away to West Götaland. Svein was king of the Swedes for three winters.

King Ingi went with his guards and a small body of soldiers, only a tiny army. He rode east through Småland and into East Götaland and then into Sweden. He rode both day and night, and came upon an unexpecting Svein early in the morning. They trapped all the people inside the house and struck up a fire and burned them. A certain man with land was named Thjóf, who burned inside; he had followed Svein before. Sacrifice-Svein emerged from the house and was immediately killed. Ingi then took the Kingdom of the Swedes for his own and led them into the true faith of Christianity, and ruled there until his death-day when he died of sickness. Hallstein, the son of King Steinkel, the brother of King Ingi, was king along with his brother King Ingi. The sons of Hallstein were Philippus and Ingi, and these two took over ruling Sweden after King Ingi the Old. Philippus married Ingigerd, the daughter of King Harald Sigurdarson. He was king only a short time.

The Saga of Hrólf Kraki
and His Champions

(Hrólfs saga kraka ok kappa hans)

Part 1: *The Tale of Fródi*

Chapter 1

A man was named Hálfdan, and another was Fródi. They were brothers and sons of a king, and each of them ruled a kingdom. King Hálfdan was gentle and forgiving and cheerful, but King Fródi was a great wild man. King Hálfdan had three children, two sons and a daughter named Signý. She was the oldest, and was married to Jarl Sævil. These events happened when his sons were still young. One of them was named Hróar, and the other Helgi. Their foster-father was named Regin, and he loved the boys very much.

There was an island that lay not far from the town. A man lived there who was named Vífil, an old friend of King Hálfdan. Vífil had two dogs; one was named Hopp and the other Hó. Vífil was wealthy and he could call up a great deal of ancient wisdom when he needed it.

Now it is said that King Fródi sat in his kingdom and he envied his brother King Hálfdan that he had the rule of Denmark on his own, but he thought his own destiny had not turned out as good. Thus, he assembled a crowd, very many people, and went to Denmark and came there under the darkness of night, burning everything and setting it to the torch. This came upon King Hálfdan with little warning. Fróði had him captured and killed, and those who were near Hálfdan fled. But all the people of the town had to swear an oath of faithfulness to King Fróði, or otherwise he would have them tortured in various ways.

Regin, the foster-father of Helgi and Hróar, got them away and brought them to an island belonging to Vífil. The boys mourned for their father Hálfdan's loss.

Regin told Vífil the boys would have no other hiding places left, if Vífil could not keep them from King Fróði. Vífil said, "Here is a difficult task," but said he would do a great deal to help the boys. So he welcomed them there, and hid them in a turf-house, and they were usually inside it overnight. But in the day they would wander Vífil's woods, because the island was half covered in forest. And in this way they parted from Regin.

Regin had great property in Denmark, and a wife and children, and thus Regin saw no other option but to submit to King Fróði and swear the oath of loyalty to him. Now King Fróði put all of the Kingdom of Denmark under his control with taxes and duties. For the most part people did not submit willingly, because King Fróði was an unpopular man, and his taxes fell also on Jarl Sævil.

And after all of this had passed, King Fróði continued to be anxious that the boys Helgi and Hróar had not been found. He ordered men to watch for them on all sides, near and far, north and south, east and west, and promised great rewards to anyone who could tell him anything about them, and tortures to anyone who discovered them but didn't say anything to the king. Then he had his men search for seeresses and wise men from all over the realm, and he ordered them to search the shores and beyond, in all the islands and skerries, and yet still the boys were not found.

Now Fróði ordered wizards brought to him, sorcerers who could find out the truth about anything. And they told him that though these two boys were not being raised in Fróði's own realm, they were not very far from the king regardless. King Fróði said, "We have searched for them widely, and I think it is implausible that they are near here. But there is an island close by, which we have not searched much. And it is hardly inhabited, though one poor man lives there."

"Look there first," said the wizards, "Because a great fog and bewilderment lies over that island, and thus we cannot easily see the house of that poor man, and we think he must be wise, and must be something more than he seems."

The king said, "Then the island will be searched. Yet it would seem strange to me if such a poor fisherman were the one keeping these boys, and dared to hide anyone from me."

Chapter 2

It was early one morning that the poor man Vífil woke up and said, "There are many strange things journeying and flying, and many mighty spirits have come to this island. Stand up, Hróar and Helgi, sons of Hálfdan! Keep yourselves in the forest today." They ran into the forest.

Now it so happened that Vífil knew that King Fróði's messengers had come onto the island and were searching for the two boys in every place it occurred to them to look.

They never found the boys, and yet they thought Vífil seemed suspicious. They left after searching the island, and told the king that they could not find them. "You must have searched badly," said the king, "and I think this man is magically talented. Go back now to that place. Take the same route, so that the man will least expect you, and he won't be able to hide them quickly if they are there."

Now they did as the king told them, and they went back a second time to the island. Vífil said to the boys, "You can't rest yet—go into the forest as fast as you can!" The boys did so, and just after this the king's men rushed to Vífil and ordered him to let them search, and he let them see everything. Yet they found nothing on the island, wherever they looked, and thus they went back after this and told the king.

King Fróði said, "Now this man won't be treated with leniency any longer. I myself will go to the island first thing in the morning." And the king did as he told, and personally went to the island the next morning. Vífil awoke in some pain and saw that he would have to come up with a new plan soon. He then said to the brothers, "You must respond if I call you Hopp and Hó, the names of my dogs. Now go to your turf-house and keep in mind that no more peace will come to this island, and you will not be safe here longer, because your kinsman Fróði is one of the searchers and he intends to end your lives with all kinds of schemes and tricks, and I do not know whether I will be able to keep you here."

Then Vífil went to the shore, and the king's ship had already arrived there. He acted as though he didn't see it, and pretended to be looking for his cattle so hard that he never looked in the direction of the king and his men. The king told his men to capture the man, and this was done and he was brought before the king.

King Fróði said, "You are a great trickster and very deceptive. Tell me where the king's sons are, because you know that."

Vífil said, "Hail, my lord! Don't hold me here, because the wolf will tear my cattle apart!" Then he shouted loudly, "Hopp and Hó, help the cattle! Now I can't help them!"

The king said, "What are you calling now?"

"My dogs are named that. But search now, my lord, as much as you like. I don't expect that the king's sons are here, and I am surprised that you think I would hide people from you."

The king said, "You are certainly a liar, but the boys won't be spared a second time, not even if they have been before. It would be fitting if I killed you."

Vífil said, "You have that right. Then at least you'd get something done on this island, rather than leave with things as they are."

The king said, "I'm not ordering you killed, though I think it is probably ill-advised that I don't." Now the king went home.

Vífil found the boys and told them that they couldn't remain there any longer. "I will send you to Sævil, your brother-in-law, and you will become famous men, if you live long."

Chapter 3

Hróar was twelve winters old at this time, and Helgi ten, but Helgi was bigger and bolder. Now they went away, and Hróar called himself Hrani and Helgi called himself Ham wherever they went or found men to speak to. These boys came to Jarl Sævil and remained there for a week before they talked about their presence with the jarl. He said, "I think there is little promise in you, but I won't deny you food for the time being." They stayed there a while and were fairly unsociable. No one knew what boys they might be, nor did anyone know their family. The jarl did not suspect the truth either, and in no way did they let him guess their true situation. Some men said that they had been born with scabies, and made fun of them because they were always dressed in hooded garments and never took the hoods off. Many suspected that they were covering up their scabs. They were there through a third winter.

On one occasion, King Fróði invited Jarl Sævil to a feast. Fróði strongly suspected now that Sævil was hiding the boys, on account of his relationship to them. The jarl prepared for the journey with a large crowd of men. The boys asked to go with him, but the jarl said they could not. Signý, the jarl's wife, was also along on the journey. Ham, who was really Helgi, found himself an untamed colt to ride. He ran now after the troop and rode backward, looking over the horse's tail and in every way acting foolishly. His brother Hrani got a horse of similar quality, but rode looking in the right direction.

Now the jarl saw that they were coming behind him and that they couldn't control their horses. The shaggy colts kept shying this way and that underneath them, and the cloak fell from Hrani's head. Their sister Signý was able to see this, and she recognized them immediately and wept very hard. The jarl asked why she cried, and she spoke this poem:

"The whole family-tree
of the Skjoldungs,
of the king of Lund,
is reduced to firewood.
I saw my brothers
riding bareback,
but Sævil's men
had saddles."

The jarl said, "This is some important news. Don't let it be revealed." Then he rode back to the boys (both of them had fallen off their mounts now) and told them to go back, as they would only be humiliated in the company of good men. And he said this because he had learned who these boys were, but he wanted no one to guess the truth from the way he spoke to them. The boys now acted as if they were going back, but they didn't intend to return to Sævil's realm, and so they continued to ride on somewhat behind the jarl's group.

The boys now came to the feast and ran back and forth around the hall. And one time they did this near where their sister Signý was. She said to them very quietly, "Don't be in this hall, because you are not old enough." They did not pay her any attention.

King Fróði began saying that he wanted the sons of Hálfdan searched for, and he said that great honor would be given to anyone who could give him some information about them.

A certain seeress [*vǫlva*] named Heið had arrived there. King Fróði asked her to use her power to find out what she could say about the boys. Then he gave her a great feast and set her up on a high scaffold for dark magic [*seiðhjallr*]. The king then asked her what kind of news she could see, "because I know," he said, "that much will be revealed to you now, and I see a great gift in you. Answer me as fast as you can, witch." Then her jaws were forced wide open and she gasped loudly, and then this song came from her mouth:

> "There are two inside
> (I don't trust either),
> they sit by fires,
> they are glorious."

The king said, "Is it the boys, or the ones who have protected them?" She said:

> "It's the ones who stayed
> on Vífil's island a long time,
> where they were known by

the names of dogs:
Hopp and Hó."

And at that moment Signý tossed the seeress a golden ring. The seeress was glad for the gift, and wanted to stop her performance. "Why did that happen?" the seeress said. "After all, this is only lies I have said, and now all my gift of prophecy departs from me."

The king said, "You will be tortured into talking, if you won't accept fine gifts. And now here I am before this crowd, and I don't know any better than before what you're talking about, or why Signý isn't in her seat, and it may be that here the wolves are in counsel with the wolves."

Someone told the king that Signý was sick from the smoke that came from the oven. Jarl Sævil asked her to sit up and carry herself proudly, "because there are many who can kill the boys if they want to. Act as though it's the last thing you'd think about, because we may not be able to help them with things as they are." King Fróði now turned his attention strongly upon the witch and told her to tell the truth if she did not want to be tortured. She then opened her mouth very wide, and the dark magic became difficult, and then she said this stanza:

"I see where the sons
of Hálfdan are sitting,
Hróar and Helgi,
in good health,
they will take
the life of Fróði,

". . . unless they are quickly killed, but that will not be," she said. And after this she vaulted herself down off the scaffold and said:

"Ham's and Hrani's eyes
are snake-like and fierce;
those boys are princes, and
wonderfully brave."

After this, the boys ran out into the woods with great fear. Regin, their foster-father, recognized them and realized this was a crucial moment. But the seeress had given them sound advice, when she said they ought to hide themselves, and then she ran out along the hall. And now the king told his men to rise and search for them. Regin then put out all the lights in the hall, and now the men disagreed, because some thought they'd gotten away into the forest, and amid all this the boys did manage to reach the woods. The king said, "They are very near now, and there are people here who must be allied and complicit with them, and this will be avenged fiercely when there is time. But now we will drink through the night. The boys will be happy that they got away, and the first thing they'll try to do is conceal themselves."

Regin went to serve drinks, and he energetically served the ale. So did many other men, friends of his, so that before long all the men were falling crossways over each other asleep.

Chapter 4

The brothers remained in the forest for now, as has been told, and when they'd been there for a while they saw that a man was riding toward them from the hall. They thought it was Regin, their foster-father, coming. They were happy to see him and greeted him well. He did not acknowledge their greeting, but turned his horse back around toward the hall. They thought this was strange and talked about what this might be about.

And now Regin turned his horse back toward them and had an unfriendly look, as if he were about to attack them right there. Helgi said, "I think we ought to hurry, whatever he intends." Then Regin went home to the hall, and they followed him. "Thus my foster-father shows," said Helgi, "that he doesn't want to break his oaths to King Fróði, and that's why he won't speak with us, but he still wants to help us."

There was a grove near the hall that the king owned, and when they reached this place, Regin said to himself: "If I had great differences with King Fróði, I would burn this grove down." He said nothing further.

Hróar said, "What does this mean?"

"It means," said Helgi, "that he wants us two to go to the hall and set it on fire except for one exit."

"How could we do that, two boys, as overpowered as we'd be?"

"It will be done, nevertheless," said Helgi, "and we must always be ready to take risks, if we're going to be able to get vengeance for our grievances." And so they did it, and soon after Jarl Sævil emerged from the burning hall with all his men.

Sævil said, "Let's build up the fire now and give some help to these boys. I have no obligation to King Fróði."

Chapter 5

King Fróði had two craftsmen, who were veritable Volunds in their skill, and both were named Var.

Regin helped his people, both his friends and his kinsmen, get out of the hall. King Fróði woke up now inside the hall and he breathed hard and said, "I've had a dream, boys, and not a good one. I'll tell it to you. I dreamed that a loud voice called to us, and someone said this: 'Now you've come home, king, you and your men.' I thought I answered, and not kindly: 'Home to where?' Then the voice came so near to me that I could feel the breath of the speaker: 'Home to Hel, home to Hel,' said the one who spoke, and I woke up to that."

And at that moment they heard Regin speaking this poem outside the hall doors:

> "Regin is outside,
> with Hálfdan's sons,
> tough enemies—
> tell it to Fróði!
> Var made the nails,
> Var hammered,
> but Var struck
> nails made by Var."

Then the king's men who were inside said that this was not big news, that Regin was outside or that the king's craftsmen would work at building, whether they made nails or other tools. The king said, "Do you think this isn't news? It might not be for us. Now Regin has told us about a certain fear, and he has given me a warning, and he will be crafty and sly in dealing with us."

Then the king went to the hall doors and saw that there were ominous events outside. Then the whole hall began to burn. King Fródi asked who started the fire. They told him that the brothers Helgi and Hróar set it. The king asked them to accept a peaceful settlement and to speak about it among themselves, "And this is an evil thing to happen between kinsmen, that one of us would be the killer of another."

Helgi answered, "No one can trust you. Wouldn't you have betrayed us no slower than you did my father Hálfdan? Now you will pay for that."

King Fródi turned away from the hall doors and into the mouth of his turf-house and he intended to go there into the forest to hide himself. And as he entered the turf-house, he found Regin there in front of him and not in a friendly mood. The king then turned back and was burned to death inside, and many of his troops along with him. Sigríd, the mother of Helgi and Hróar, burned there, because she did not want to go out.

The brothers thanked Jarl Sævil, their brother-in-law, for his good help, as well as their foster-father Regin, and they thanked all the men and gave them good gifts. They now took over the kingdom and all the property, land, and money that King Fródi had owned. In their temperament, the brothers were not alike. Hróar was a mild and kind man, and Helgi was a great warrior, and he seemed better at everything. And now time passed for a while. And here ends the Tale of Fródi, and here begins the tale of Hróar and Helgi, the sons of Hálfdan.

Part 2: *The Tale of Helgi*

Chapter 6

A king was named Norðri, and his daughter was named Ogn. Norðri ruled over a certain part of England. Hróar spent a long time with King Norðri, assisting him with guarding and strengthening his land, and there was great friendship between them. And later Hróar married Ogn and became co-ruler with King Norðri, his father-in-law, while Helgi ruled Denmark, which was the inheritance from their father.

Jarl Sævil ruled over his domain with Signý. Hrók was the name of their son.

King Helgi, the son of Hálfdan, king of Denmark, was unmarried. Regin became ill and died. This seemed a great shame to men, because he was so popular.

Chapter 7

A queen named Ólof ruled over Saxony in that time. She led her life in the way of war-kings; she went around with a shield and armor, with a sword in her belt and a helmet on her head. This was her way: she was beautiful in appearance, but grim and arrogant in behavior. It was said by men that, of all women anyone had heard tell of during that time in the Northlands, she would be the best choice in marriage, but she wanted to marry no man.

Now King Helgi learned of this arrogant queen, and he thought that his fame would increase a great deal if he could marry her, whether she was more or less willing to marry him.

On one occasion he traveled with a great army. He came to the land where this powerful queen ruled, and did so with her unaware. He sent men to her hall and told them to say to Queen Ólof that he wanted to be treated to a feast there with his army. The messengers told the queen this, and it came upon her by surprise, and she had no chance to assemble her own defensive force. So she chose what was better, and she invited King Helgi and all his army to a feast.

Then King Helgi came to the feast and took a throne near the queen, and they drank together during the evening. There was no shortage of anything, and no trace of unhappiness on Queen Ólof's face. King Helgi told her, "It so happens that I want us to celebrate our wedding together this evening. There is enough of a crowd here for it, and the two of us will share one bed tonight."

She said, "This seems done too soon, lord, though I don't think any other man is nobler than you (if I must compare men). But I think that you will not want to do this with dishonor."

King Helgi said that she would deserve it on account of her arrogance and pride, "That we now dwell together for whatever length of time I like."

She said, "I would choose to have more of my friends here, but I can do nothing. You will have to decide. You will do honorably to me."

Then there was a great deal of drinking during the evening and long into the night, and the queen was very cheerful, and no one could see any sign from her except that she was very happy with the decision. And later when King Helgi was guided to bed, she was already there. The king had drunk so much that he immediately fell asleep when he lay down. The queen was pleased with this, and stung him with a sleep-thorn.

And when all the men had left them there, the queen stood up. First she shaved all of Helgi's hair off and rubbed him all over with tar, then she took a bag made of animal hide and put some of his clothes in it, and then took the king and stuffed him inside of this bag among the loose clothing. Then she went to her men and had them take King Helgi to his ships. Then she woke up Helgi's men and told them that their king had gone to his ships and wanted to sail, because a good wind had come up. They leapt up as fast as they could, and they were all very drunk and barely knew what was going on. Then they went to the ships and did not see the king, but they did see that there was a large, ugly bag made of animal hide. They were curious as to what might be in the bag, yet they waited for the king, thinking he would come a little later. But when they finally did open up the bag, they found inside of it their king, and they saw how treacherously he had been betrayed.

Then one of them flicked the sleep-thorn away. The king awoke now, and not from a good dream. He felt great malice for the queen.

As to Queen Ólof, she assembled her army during the night, and she did not lack for troops, and King Helgi saw that this was not his opportunity to attack her. Now they heard a trumpet blow and the sound of a summons for the army up on the land, and the king saw that the most prudent option was to get away as fast as possible. There was also a good breeze. So King Helgi sailed away home to his kingdom with disgrace and shame, and he liked this very little.

Helgi often thought about how he might get his revenge on the queen.

Chapter 8

Now Queen Ólof sat for a while in her kingdom, and her arrogance and pride had never been greater than now. She kept a strong force of men stationed around her to watch at all times, after the feast that she had given King Helgi.

This was told widely across all lands. Everyone thought that it was truly appalling that she had mocked such a king.

Not much later, King Helgi sailed his ship from home, and on this journey he came to Saxony where Queen Ólof ruled. She had a large army gathered to defend the coastline. But Helgi sailed his ship into a hidden cove and then told his men that they were to wait for him there until the third sun had come, and then they were to leave if he had not come back. He had with him two treasure chests full of gold and silver. He then put poor clothing on over his own.

Helgi went alone into the forest and there he stashed his money, and then he went to the proximity of the queen's hall. He met a slave of hers there and asked him the news, saying that he had come from other lands. The slave told him that there was peace in the land, and he asked who this man was. He said he was a beggar, "but it so happens that I have made a great discovery of money out in the forest, and I thought it would be advisable to let you know where that money is." Then he went back to the forest and showed the slave where the money was, and the slave thought this was worth a great deal, whatever else had happened in his life.

"How greedy is the queen?" asked the beggar.

The slave said she was the greediest of all women.

"Then she will like this," said the beggar, "and she will decide she owns this money, because this is her land. Now I don't want to make my good luck into bad—I won't hide this money, and the queen will give me what she thinks I deserve out of it. And that will be the best thing for me. Will she want to come see this money here herself?"

"I think so," said the slave, "If everything is done secretly."

"Here is a necklace and a ring that I want to give you," said the man, "If you can bring her into the forest here alone. And I will help you out, if she doesn't like you at first impression." They agreed to this and the deal was made.

Then the slave went home and told the queen that he had found a great deal of money in the forest, so much that it would be a comfort for many men, and he asked her to go with him in haste to the money. She said, "If what you say is true, then your prize will be either your fortune or your decapitation. But because I have previously known you to be a truth-telling man, I will trust what you say." In this way she showed how greedy she was.

Now the queen went with him in secret during the dark of night, so that no one knew except these two. And when they came into the forest, there was Helgi before them and he grabbed the queen in his hands and said this would be a fitting occasion to avenge her betrayal.

The queen admitted that she had behaved evilly toward him, "And now I want to make it up to you, King Helgi. And for your part, marry me with honor."

"No," he said, "you won't have any choice in this. You will go to my ships with me and stay there a while, as long as I like, because for the sake of my good name I don't want you to get away with this unpunished, as evilly and mockingly as you treated me."

"It will have to be you who decides this, as you please," she said.

The king slept with the queen many nights. And after this the queen went home. Her wrong deeds had been avenged in the way just told, and she was very displeased with her situation.

Chapter 9

After this, King Helgi went raiding. He was a great man.

And after some time had passed, Queen Ólof gave birth to a girl. She treated the girl with great indifference, and named her Yrsa after a dog she had owned named Yrsa.

The girl was, however, beautiful. And when she reached twelve years old, she was forced to herd sheep, and she never knew that she was anything other than the daughter of a poor farmer and his poor wife, because the queen had concealed her pregnancy such that only a few men knew that she had even given birth to a child at all.

Things proceeded in this way until the girl was thirteen years old. Then it so happened that King Helgi came to the land and was curious to hear some news of the place. He traveled again in a beggar's clothing. In a certain forest he saw a large flock of sheep, and it was herded by a very young girl who was so beautiful that he thought he'd never seen a more beautiful woman. He asked her what she was named and what family she was from.

She said, "I am a farmer's daughter, and my name is Yrsa."

"You don't have peasants' eyes," he said, and he was consumed with desire for her and said that it would be fitting if she became a beggar's wife, if she was a poor farmer's daughter.

She asked him not to do this, but he took her captive and brought her to his ships, as he had Queen Ólaf before, and then sailed home to his kingdom.

Queen Ólof's intent was deceitful and unwholesome in all of this. She acted as if she did not know what had happened, and it occurred to her that this might bring King Helgi sorrow and disgrace, and certainly no fame or joy.

Now King Helgi married Yrsa, and loved her very much.

Chapter 10

King Helgi had a famous ring. He and his brother Hróar both wanted it, as did their sister Signý.

One time King Hróar came to the kingdom of his brother Helgi, and King Helgi greeted him with a splendid feast.

King Hróar said, "You will be the more important man of the two of us, but because I have established myself in Northumberland, I won't grudge you the rule of this kingdom that we hold together here, as long as you will share some more movable property with me. I want the ring, which is the best treasure you own, and the two of us will both always desire it."

Helgi answered, "Nothing is appropriate, kinsman, except to let you have that ring."

And after these remarks, they both became more cheerful, and King Helgi gave his brother King Hróar the ring. And now King Hróar went away to his kingdom and sat there in peace.

Chapter 11

The time came that their brother-in-law Sævil died, and Sævil's son Hrók took over his kingdom after him. He was a tough man and very ambitious. His mother told Hrók much about the ring that the brothers Helgi and Hróar owned. "And I don't think," she said, "that it's unlikely at all that the brothers will repay us with some part of their wealth, because we assisted them when they avenged our father. But thus far they have repaid neither your father nor me."

Hrók said, "You speak the absolute truth, and this is a shameful matter. And now I will find out what honor they'll give us for this."

Then Hrók journeyed to visit King Helgi, and asked him for a third of the kingdom of Denmark, or for that good ring—because he did not know that Hróar had it.

Helgi said, "You speak very arrogantly, dangerously so even. We won your kingdom for you with heroic actions, and we laid our lives down as wagers with the assistance of your father, and my foster-father Regin, and other good men who wanted to join us. Now we certainly would wish to give you gifts, if you can accept them, because of our kinship. But this kingdom has cost me so much that I will not give it up for any reason. And it's Hróar who has the ring now, and I don't think that he's careless with it."

With this, Hrók went away feeling very unhappy, and he went to meet King Hróar. Hróar greeted him well with honor, and Hrók stayed there a while with him. And one time, when they left the land and were in a certain fjord, Hrók said, "It seems to me that it would give you honor, kinsman, if you gave me the good ring and in this way remembered our kinship."

King Hróar said, "I have given so much in order to own this ring, that nothing will make me give it up."

Hrók said, "Then you must promise to let me see the ring, as I have an immense curiosity to know whether it is as good a treasure as it is said to be."

"That is only a little favor to grant you," said Hróar, "and I'll certainly do that." Now he brought him the ring. Hrók looked at the ring a little while and said that what men said about it was no exaggeration, "And I have never seen such a treasure, and it is very understandable that you think so much of the ring. It would be the wisest course of action, if neither you nor I enjoyed it, nor anyone else," and he flung the ring from his hand and out into the sea, as far as he could.

King Hróar said, "You are a thoroughly bad man." Then he had Hrók's feet cut off, and ordered his men to carry him back to his own kingdom.

Hrók soon healed in such a way that the stumps grew over, and then he summoned an army and wished to avenge his shame. He put together a large force and attacked Northumberland by surprise, during a time when King Hróar was at a feast with only a few men. Hrók attacked directly, and there was a hard battle, though one side was much larger. King Hróar died there, and Hrók took over the kingdom.

Hrók now took the name of king, and he proposed for the hand of Ogn, the daughter of King Norðri and the widow of his kinsman King Hróar. King Norðri thought this was a difficult dilemma facing him, because he had grown old and now had little ability in battle. He told his daughter Ogn how things stood, and said he would not hesitate to offer battle in return, no matter how old he was, if this marriage would be against her wishes. She said, in agony, "This is certainly against my wishes, but I also see clearly that your life is at stake. Still

I will not refuse him as long as a little delay is allowed, because I am pregnant with the child of King Hróar. And first I must give birth to this child." Now this answer was presented to Hrók, and he agreed to allow the delay, because he would become even richer in property and dominion after the marriage.

Hrók thought he had gained great fame in this journey, because he had killed such a famous king and won a kingdom.

And during this delay in time, Ogn sent messengers to King Helgi and told them to inform him that she would not come into the bed of Hrók, if she had her own choice and was not forced to do so, "Because I am pregnant with the child of King Hróar."

The messengers went and told King Helgi what they had been instructed to say. King Helgi said, "She has spoken wisely, because I will avenge my brother Hróar." And Hrók suspected nothing.

Chapter 12

Now Queen Ogn gave birth to a son named Agnar. He was soon big and promising. And when King Helgi learned this, he assembled an army and went to meet Hrók. There was a battle, and it ended with the capture of Hrók.

Now King Helgi said, "You are a thoroughly evil leader, but I will not kill you because it is a greater shame for you to live with such anguishing wounds. Then he had Hrók's arms and legs broken, and sent him back into his own kingdom, capable of nothing.

And when Agnar, the son of Hróar, turned twelve years old, men said they had never seen such a man, as he was the superior of every man in every kind of undertaking. He became such an important and famous warrior that he is widely remembered in ancient sagas as the greatest champion then or now.

One time Agnar asked where the fjord was where Hrók had thrown the ring overboard. Many had searched for the ring with all kinds of tricks, and no one had found it. And it is said that Agnar arrived at this fjord in his ship and said, "It would be a good idea to look for the ring, if someone had a clear idea where to fish for it."

Then he was told where it had been cast into the sea. Agnar prepared himself and dived into the depths. When he came back up, he did not have the ring. Then he went down a second time, and again he did not have the ring when he came back up. Now he said, "I've been lazy about looking," and he went down a third time and came back up with the ring. Because of this, he became extraordinarily famous, more so than his father King Hróar. Now Agnar stayed in his kingdom during the winters, and went on Viking raids during the summers, and became a legendary man, and he was considered greater than his father.

For their part, King Helgi and Yrsa loved each other very much and had one son named Hrólf, who later would become a man of great reputation.

Chapter 13

Now Queen Ólof learned that Helgi and Yrsa loved each other very much and were content with their lives, and she did not like this. She went to visit them, and when she came into the land she sent word to Queen Yrsa.

When Ólof and Yrsa met, Yrsa invited her home to the royal hall with her, but Ólof said she did not want to go there, because she came with no joy to repay to King Helgi.

Yrsa said, "You treated me unworthily, when I was with you. Can you tell me something of my ancestors—who are they? For I suspect that it might not be true that I am the daughter of a poor farmer and his wife, which is what I was told."

Ólof said, "It's not a surprise if I'm the one who can give you some of the answer. It was the most important part of my errand in coming here, to make you aware of it. Do you like the way you're living now?"

"Yes," said Yrsa, "and it's sensible that I do, because I am married to the greatest and most famous of all kings."

"It isn't as sensible to be happy about this as you think it is," said Ólof, "Because he is your father, and I am your mother."

Yrsa said, "I think my mother is the worst and the cruelest of all mothers, because there is no outrage equal to this, and it will be notorious forever."

"You have repaid Helgi for his part in this," said Ólof, "and satisfied my anger. Now I want to invite you home with me, to live in honor and grace, and I will treat you in the best manner possible, in every way."

Yrsa said, "I don't know how that will go, but I cannot remain in this home now that I know the evil that is part of it."

Then Yrsa went to King Helgi and told him what a bad end everything had come to. Hrólf said, "You had a mother with plenty of evil in her, but it is my desire that things stay as they are."

But Yrsa said that they could no longer live together after this, and she went home with Queen Ólof to Saxony for a while. This affected King Helgi so much that he laid a long time in bed and remained completely in misery.

It was agreed by everyone that there was no better choice in women than Yrsa, but other kings were reluctant to ask for her hand. And the biggest reason for this was fear that Helgi would go after her and spread his suffering around if she married someone else.

Chapter 14

There was a king named Adils, who was rich and greedy, and who ruled Sweden from his capital at Uppsala. He learned about Yrsa and prepared his ships, then journeyed to meet Ólof and Yrsa. Ólof greeted King Adils with a feast, and he was treated to every art and courtesy.

Adils asked for the hand of Queen Yrsa in marriage. Ólof answered, "Certainly you have heard of what her situation is, but I will not deny her to you if she agrees to it."

The matter was then presented to Yrsa, who said she thought it was a bad match, "Because you are an unpopular king." But the marriage went forward anyway, whether Yrsa wanted to speak for it or against it, and Adils went home with her. King Helgi was not asked for his consent, because Adils thought Helgi was the lesser king. King Helgi did not become aware of the arrangement until Adils and Yrsa had reached Sweden, where Adils married Yrsa in a worthy ceremony.

It was now that King Helgi learned of this, and became half again as angry as he had been previously. He slept in a small hut outside, with no one else near.

Now Ólof is out of the saga, but things continued in this way for a while.

Chapter 15

It is told that one Yule Eve, King Helgi had gone to bed and the weather was bad outside. There was a knock at the door that spoke to great strength in the one knocking, and it occurred to the king that it would be unkingly for him to leave the poor beggar outside, and that he ought to save whoever it was.

He went and opened the door, and it was a poor woman dressed in rags that he saw there. The beggar woman said, "You have done well now, king," and came into the hut.

The king said "Pull some of the straw and bear-pelts over you, so that you don't get chilled."

The beggarwoman said, "Let me have your bed, my lord, and I will sleep beside you. Otherwise my life is at risk."

The king said, "This stretches my generosity, but if it is as you say, then lie down here on the edge of the bed in your clothes, and I won't grudge you that." She did so.

Now the king turned away from her, and a light flashed inside the hut. And after a little time passed, he happened to see her out of the corner of his eye, and he saw that a woman was resting there, dressed in a silk gown, who was so beautiful that he thought he had never seen one more beautiful. Now he rushed up to this woman eagerly.

"I want to go away now," she said. "You have released me from a terrible curse, which was the work of my stepmother, and I have visited the homes of many kings before you. Now don't follow a good deed with a bad one; I want to go away now and not stay here any longer."

"No," said the king, "you don't have a choice in that. You can't go so soon, and we aren't going to part like this. Now I'm going to marry you quickly, because I like the look of you."

"It is yours to decide, lord," she said, and they slept together that night. But then in the morning she said, "You have acted toward me with lust alone, and you ought to know that we will have a child together. Do as I tell you, king, visit our child in the second winter from now at this same time, in your boat-house. You will pay for it if you do not." After this she went away.

Now King Helgi was more cheerful than before. Some time passed without him giving it much thought. But in the third winter it happened that three people rode to the same house that the king slept in at around midnight. They came with an infant girl and set her down beside the house.

The woman who held the baby said, "You ought to know, king, that your descendants will pay a price for how you disregarded what I said to you. But you will have some joy of the fact that you freed me from my curse. Know this, that this girl is named Skuld, and she is your and my daughter." After this, these people rode away. The woman had been an elf-woman, and the king never saw her again.

Now Skuld grew up there, and soon she was cruel in disposition. It is said that one time, King Helgi prepared to journey away from the land and distract himself from his anguish, and his son Hrólf stayed behind. King Helgi now raided widely, and did many great things.

Chapter 16

King Aðils remained in Uppsala. He had twelve berserkers who guarded his land from every danger and conflict.

Now King Helgi prepared his expedition to go to Uppsala and take back Yrsa. He arrived in Sweden, and when King Aðils learned that Helgi was there, he asked Queen Yrsa how he ought to greet King Helgi.

She said, "You know the proper answer to that, but you knew already that there is no man I have a closer relationship to than to him."

And it seemed to King Adils that it was right to invite Helgi to a feast, but he did not think it ought to be an invitation without some fraud in it. King Helgi anticipated this and went to the feast with a hundred men, leaving most of them in the ships nearby. King Adils greeted Helgi with both hands. Queen Yrsa intended to make some settlement between the kings, and she treated King Helgi with great honor. For his part, King Helgi was so glad to see Yrsa that he paid no attention to anything else. He wanted to spend all the time he could talking to her, and this is how it went all throughout the feast.

It so happened that this was when the berserkers of King Adils came home. And when they had come home to Sweden, King Adils went to greet them secretly, so that others were not aware. He told them to go into the forest between the city and King Helgi's ships, and told them to attack King Helgi from there when he went to his ships. "And I will send you some reinforcements, and they will come at them from behind so that they'll be pinned in, because I want to be certain that King Helgi cannot get away. He is so in love with the queen that I don't want to risk some ingenious maneuver by him."

Meanwhile King Helgi was sitting at the feast and was completely unaware of this treacherous plan, as was Queen Yrsa. She sent a message to King Adils, asking him to give King Helgi some nobleman's gifts, gold and treasures. He promised this, but he intended the gifts for himself instead. Now King Helgi began to leave, and King Adils and Queen Yrsa followed him out to the road, and that is where they parted. And not long after King Adils had disappeared from view, King Helgi and his men became aware of the men waiting in ambush, and then the battle began.

King Helgi made a good advance forward, and he fought hard, but because of the superior numbers that faced him there, King Helgi died there with a good reputation and many large wounds.

Some of his army came back to King Adils, and they were caught as if between a rock and a hammer. Queen Yrsa knew nothing about it before King Helgi was dead and the battle was over.

It was here that Helgi died with all his army that had traveled with him, and the rest returned home to Denmark. Here the story of King Helgi ends.

Chapter 17

Now King Adils praised the victory and thought that he had become much more famous, because he had defeated a king as great and widely famed as Helgi had been. But Queen Yrsa said, "There is no clear reason to boast so much, even if you have betrayed the man who was most closely related of all to me, and who of all men was my greatest love. And because of this, I will never be loyal to you if you attack King Helgi's relations. I will cause the deaths of your berserkers, whichever ones I can, if any one of Helgi's kinsmen is so brave that he will attack us for my sake and his own manhood's."

King Adils told her not to promise such things about him or his berserkers, "Because it won't help you. But I will compensate you for your father's death with a great deal of money and with good treasures, if you will accept them." The queen calmed down when she heard this, and she accepted honor from the king.

But Yrsa was now uneasy in her mind, and she often sat and thought about how to do some harm or shame to the berserkers. Adils's men never again found Queen Yrsa cheerful or in a good mood after the death of King Helgi, and there was more disagreement in the king's hall than there had been before, and Queen Yrsa would not settle peacefully with King Adils if she had any say over a matter.

For King Adils's part, he thought he had become very famous, and anyone who came among the king and his great champions was considered the greatest of men. For a while he stayed in his kingdom and thought that no one would dare attack him or his berserkers.

King Adils was a man who made many sacrifices, and he was very knowledgeable in magic.

Part 3: The Tale of Svipdag

Chapter 18

There was a wealthy farmer named Svip, who lived in Sweden far from other men. He was very rich, and he had been the greatest of champions, and not only in matters where witnesses had seen him. He was also very wise. He had three sons, and their names were Svipdag, Beigaḋ, and Hvítserk. Hvítserk was the oldest. All of Svip's sons were large men, strong and handsome.

And when Svipdag was eighteen years old, he told his father one day, "It is a waste of our lives to be up here in the mountains in remote valleys, never visiting other people or being visited by other people. It would be a better idea to go to King Aḋils and be in his district with him and his champions, if he would receive us."

Svip answered, "This doesn't seem advisable to me, because King Aḋils is a cruel man and not well in mind, even if he does speak fairly. And his men are jealous, though great, and certainly King Aḋils is a powerful and wealthy man."

Svipdag said, "I'll have to take a risk, if I want to get some fame. And I won't know until I try just which way my luck will turn. And I certainly won't sit here any longer, whatever else is destined for me."

And because he had decided on this venture, Svip gave him a large ax, beautiful and sharp. And then he said to his son, "Do not be greedy with others, and don't behave arrogantly, because that will get you a bad reputation. And defend yourself, if someone attacks you, because it is not the habit of great men to puff themselves up, but to earn a great reputation if they are faced with some kind of test." Then he gave Svipdag the most excellently constructed armor, and a good horse.

Now Svipdag rode away, and in the evening he came to King Aḋils's fortress, where he saw that games were being held outside the king's hall where King Aḋils sat on a great golden throne with his berserkers seated around him.

And when Svipdag came to the surrounding fence, he found the gate locked, because it was the custom then to ask for permission to enter. Svipdag didn't bother with this, but just broke open the gate and rode right in.

King Aḋils said, "This man is riding uncarefully, and no one has tried such a thing before. It may be that he's as tough as he looks, but he still might not be able to deliver what he's trying to."

The berserkers frowned deeply at Svipdag, and thought he was acting dangerously arrogant. But Svipdag rode right in front of the king and greeted him well, as he knew how to do in the proper style. The king asked him who he was, and Svipdag told him. The king recognized him right away then, and everyone thought he would be the greatest of champions and a man of great deeds. The games were still going on, and Svipdag sat down on a tree and watched them.

The berserkers looked at Svipdag unhappily, and now they told the king that they were going to test him. The king said, "I don't think he lacks toughness, but it seems to me a good idea for you to find out if he is what he seems to be."

Now men came into the hall, and the berserkers came to Svipdag and asked him whether he was any kind of fighter, because he acted like such a tough man. Svipdag said that he was just like any one of them. And when he said this, their anger and aggressiveness rose in response, but the king told them to stay calm during the evening. The berserkers frowned, and howled loudly, and said to Svipdag, "Do you dare to fight us? If you do, you'll need more than tough words and a tough attitude, and we want to test just how much of a man you are."

Svipdag said, "I'll agree to fight one of you at a time, and then we'll see if more want to join in."

The king thought it was fine if these men wanted to test each other, but Queen Yrsa said, "This man ought to be welcome here."

The berserkers answered her, "We already know that you want all of us in Hel, but we are tougher than the kind of men who would die from just words, or from ill will alone."

The queen said that nothing would come of it if the king tested them how he wanted, "Considering what men you are, men he trusts as much as he does."

The leader of the berserkers then said, "I will settle you and settle your arrogance down, and show you that we are unafraid of him."

Chapter 19

And in the morning there was a hard-fought duel between Svipdag and one of the berserkers, and there was no shortage of strong blows. Every man could see that this newcomer knew how to make a sword cut with a great deal of force, and the berserker kept falling back before him, before finally Svipdag killed him there. And immediately another berserker wanted to kill Svipdag in revenge, and it went much the same way, and Svipdag did not let up before he had killed four of them in this way.

Then King Aðils said, "You have done severe damage to me, and now you're going to have to pay for it," and he told his men to stand up and kill Svipdag.

In another place the queen had assembled her own force of men, which she wanted to use to help Svipdag, and she told King Aðils that he could see how much more value there was in this one man than in all the berserkers. So the queen made a truce with them, and everyone considered Svipdag to be a greatly accomplished man.

Now Svipdag sat on the second bench facing the king, on the recommendation of Queen Yrsa.

And when the night came, Svipdag looked around and thought he still had not done enough to get back at the berserkers, and he wanted to face them again. He thought it was likely that they would attack him if they saw him alone. And it went as he predicted, because they immediately fell into fighting right there. And then the king showed up after they had fought a little while, and separated them.

After this had happened, the king outlawed the remaining berserkers because all of them had fought against one single man, and he said that he hadn't been aware earlier of just what meager men they were, outside of their tough words. The berserkers went away, but swore that they would raid in Aðils's kingdom.

The king acted as if he didn't care about the berserkers' threats, and said there was no kind of courage in these dogs. So they departed in shame and disgrace.

But in fact it was King Aðils who had egged the berserkers on to attack and kill Svipdag in the first place, when they had seen Svipdag walking alone out of the hall. He had intended to avenge himself on Svipdag in this way, without the queen becoming aware of it. But it was Svipdag who had killed one of the berserkers when the king had come to separate the fighters. King Aðils now told Svipdag not to serve the king's interests any less than all the berserkers had together, "Especially because the queen wants you to serve in the place of the berserkers." So Svipdag remained there for a time.

Chapter 20

A little later, it was reported to King Adils that the berserkers had assembled a large army and were raiding his land. King Adils now commanded Svipdag to rise up against the berserkers, saying it was his duty and that he would provide Svipdag with as large an army as he might need. Svipdag did not feel like being in charge of the army. Nonetheless, he agreed to go with the king wherever he wanted to go, but the king insisted that he take charge.

Svipdag said, "Then I ask for the lives of twelve men as my price, at a time of my choice."

The king said, "I'll grant you that." And after this Svipdag went to battle with a great army, and the king stayed home. Svipdag had booby traps made, and he threw them down where the battlesite was marked off, and he had many other tricks up his sleeve too. Then a battle began, and a hard one, and the army of the berserkers fell back and recognized they were losing when they hit the booby traps. One of the berserkers was killed, and much of their army, and those who survived fled to their ships and sailed away.

Now Svipdag came home to King Adils, and he had a victory to brag about. King Adils thanked him well for his initiative and for defending the land. Queen Yrsa said, "The seat where Svipdag sits is certainly better occupied than it was when your berserkers sat in it!" The king said this was true.

After they got away, the berserkers then assembled a new army, and they raided anew in King Adils's country. And once again the king urged Svipdag to go against them and said he would offer him full control of the army. Svipdag went to war with one-third the number of troops the berserkers had, and King Adils swore to come to the battle himself with his bodyguards. This time, Svipdag had moved quicker than the berserkers expected. When they met, there was a hard battle. For his part, King Adils assembled an army and meant to come against the berserkers by surprise on their flank.

Chapter 21

The saga now turns to the farmer Svip. He awoke one time from his sleep, breathing heavily, and he said to his two sons, "Your brother Svipdag seems to need some help, because he's in the middle of a battle not far from here and he has the smaller army. He has already lost one eye, and he has many other injuries too, though he's killed three berserkers and there are still three left."

The brothers reacted quickly and armed themselves, going straight to where the battle was. There they saw that the berserkers had an army half again as large as Svipdag's. By this point, Svipdag had accomplished a great deal, but he was badly injured and he had lost one eye. His army was being killed in huge numbers, and the king had not come to assist him.

And as the brothers came into the battle, they pushed forward hard and soon came to where the berserkers stood before them. The fight ended with all the berserkers falling at the brothers' hands. Now there began to be a great loss of life in the berserkers' army, and the brothers proved victorious, and took the survivors as prisoners.

After this, they went to meet with King Adils and told him all the news. The king thanked them well for their courageous deeds.

Svipdag had taken two wounds on his hands, and a large wound on his head, and he was one-eyed for the rest of his life. For a while he lay in bed and let his wounds heal, and Queen Yrsa cared for him. And when Svipdag had recovered to normal health, he told King Adils that he wished to go away. "I want to visit a king who will give me more honor than you do, king. You have repaid me badly for the defense of your kingdom, and such a victory as we have won for you." King Adils told him to stay home, and that he would reward him and his brothers richly, and he said that no one would be honored above them. But Svipdag said he did not want to do anything but ride away, and mostly because King Adils had not come to the recent battle before it was over because he would have been equally pleased, whoever would win the victory.

The king had, in fact, stayed in a certain forest and watched the battle from there, with a choice of entering the fray whenever he wanted, and indeed it would not have mattered to him even if Svipdag had lost the battle and died there.

Chapter 22

Now the brothers prepared to go away, and there was nothing that could hold them there. King Adils asked where they intended to go, and they answered that they had not drawn any conclusions about that—"But we will part from you at once. And now I want to get to know the ways of other men and other kings, and not grow old here in Sweden."

Now they went to their horses, and they thanked Queen Yrsa well for the honor she had given Svipdag. They mounted up on their horses and rode along their way until they came to their father. They asked him for some advice on what they ought to do, "And where should we go?"

Their father Svip said that the greatest honor would be to go among King Hrólf and his champions in Denmark. "And that is the most likely place for you to win some fame to back up your pride, because I have heard it for a fact that all the best champions in the Northlands have gathered there."

"What kind of man is he?" said Svipdag.

His father said, "I am told that King Hrólf is generous with large gifts, faithful to his promises, and a great chooser of friends, such that no man can be called his equal. He does not hold back any gold or jewels from almost anyone who might want them. He is short in height, but a big and difficult man to test, and the handsomest of men. He is proud to the arrogant, but kind and magnanimous to the poor, and to all who do not resist his rule. He is the least haughty of all men, so that he answers little men in the same way as he answers the powerful. He is such a great man that his name will never be forgotten while the world is inhabited. He also receives taxes from all other kings in his vicinity, because all of them are eager to serve him."

Svipdag said, "You've told quite a story here, and I've decided to go with both my brothers to meet King Hrólf, if he'll take us."

The farmer Svip said, "It's your business to decide your journeys and your actions, but it would seem best to me if you stayed at home with me."

They said that this would not do. So they told their father and their mother farewell, and they rode away until they came to King Hrólf. Svipdag went before the king and greeted him, and the king asked who he was. Svipdag told him his name and the names of his brothers, and he said he had been with King Aðils for a while.

King Hrólf said, "Why did you come here? There is no friendship between Aðils and my men."

Svipdag said, "I know it, lord. But still I wanted to be a man in your service, if there was a choice in the matter, as did my brothers, though you might find little remarkable about us."

The king said, "I hadn't been intending to make friends with any of King Aðils's men. But since you sought me out, I will receive you. I think it will go better for the man who doesn't reject you, because I see that you are worthy gentlemen. I have heard that you have won great fame, and killed King Aðils's berserkers and done many other courageous deeds."

"Where would you have me sit?" asked Svipdag.

The king said, "Sit next to the man named Bjálki, and let there be a space twelve men wide between the two of you and me."

Svipdag had promised King Aðils, before he left Sweden, to visit him again.

And now the brothers went to the spot which the king had directed them to. Svipdag asked Bjálki why there would be a space of twelve men between them and the king, and Bjálki said that the king's twelve berserkers sat there when they came home, but they were now out raiding.

One of King Hrólf's daughters was named Skúr ["Rain-shower," a common poetic circumlocution for "battle"], and the other Drífa ["Heavy-snowstorm," another commonplace poetic name for "battle"]. Drífa was at home with the king and she was the noblest of all women. Drífa liked the brothers, and they all got along well.

Time passed through the rest of the summer, until the berserkers came home during the fall to the king's hall. And in their usual way, they each came up to every man when they came into the hall, and each one asked every man whether he thought he was an even match for him. Men looked for the right words to answer with, words that would not hurt their honor, but nonetheless it could be heard in the words of each man who replied, that he thought he was lacking quite a bit to be an even match for the berserker. And now a berserker came to Svipdag, and asked him whether he thought he might be his match.

Svipdag sprang up and drew his sword and said he was in no way a lesser man than the berserker. The berserker said, "So swing that at my helmet." Svipdag did so, and the sword did not pierce it. Now they were about to fight, but the king ran in the middle of them and told them this was forbidden and that the two of them would be called evenly matched from then on. "And both of you will be called my friends." And after this the two men settled peacefully and were always together, going on raids and winning victories wherever they went.

King Hrólf now sent men to Sweden to meet his mother Queen Yrsa and ask her to send him the treasure that his father King Helgi had possessed and that King Aðils had taken for his own when Helgi had been killed. Yrsa said this was an appropriate request, and quite right, if only it were possible for her to do. "But if you search for the treasure yourself, I will help you faithfully, my son. King Aðils is such a greedy man that he does not care what he has to do to keep it," and she told the messengers to say this to King Hrólf, and she sent wonderful gifts also.

Chapter 23

King Hrólf now went out raiding, and it was some time before he went to meet with King Aðils. He gathered a great deal of men, and he taxed all the kings he met, and it was a great sign that all the best champions wanted to be with him and serve no other king, because he was much more generous with his money than any other king.

King Hrólf established his capital at the place called Lejre; it is in Denmark, and it is a great, strong city. There was more splendor there, more opulence, and more of everything great than in any other place, and more than anyone had heard of.

A powerful king was named Hjorvarð. He married Skuld, King Hrólf's sister and the daughter of King Helgi, with the permission of King Aðils and Queen Yrsa as well as of her brother Hrólf. On one occasion King Hrólf invited his brother-in-law Hjorvarð to a festival. One day during this festival, the two kings were outside when King Hrólf took off his belt, and handed the sword that was in it to King Hjorvarð. And when King Hrólf had put the belt back on, he took the sword back and said to King Hjorvarð, "Both of us know that it's been a saying for a long time, that the man who holds another's sword while he adjusts his belt is the lesser man. Now you must be my under-king, and endure it as well as others do." Hjorvarð became extremely angry about this but had no choice in the matter, and so he went home afterward and resented his lot.

Nonetheless, he paid taxes to King Hrólf like his other under-kings who owed him obedience. And here ends the tale of Svipdag.

Part 4: The Tale of Boðvar

Chapter 24

It is now time to recount that to the north in Norway, at Uppdalir, a king named Hring ruled. He had a son who was named Bjorn. It is now told that the queen died, and this seemed a great loss to the king and to many others besides. The king's countrymen and counselors urged him to marry again, and it happened that he sent men south through the country to court a wife for him. But these men encountered unfavorable winds and great storms, and they had to turn the prows of their ships and fight to resist the wind, and it ended with them wrecking to the north in Finnmark. They stayed there over the winter.

One day they went up on the land and came to a certain house. There were two women sitting inside, both beautiful. The women greeted them well and asked where they had come from. They told the women about their journey and what their errand was. They asked what kind of women they were and why they were there alone, so far from other people, especially such beautiful and lovely women as they were. The older woman replied, "There is a reason for all of it, boys; we are here because a powerful king courted my daughter, but she did not want to marry him. And he promised her tough penalties for this, and thus I have hidden her in this place, while her father is away from home on raids."

They asked who her father was, and her mother replied, "She is the daughter of the king of the Sámi." They asked what she was named. The older one replied, "I am named Ingibjorg, and my daughter is named Hvít. I am the concubine of the king of the Sámi." There was also a girl there acting as their servant. The king's men looked upon them well, and they agreed among themselves to ask if Hvít might come with them and be married to King Hring. It was the man in charge who brought it up with her. She did not answer quickly, but turned to her mother for a prediction.

"It is just like they say, for every difficulty some kind of solution will emerge," said her mother, "though it seems bad to me that her father is not here to be asked. But it must be risked, if she is going to get closer to a good life."

After this, Hvít prepared for her journey with them, and they went their way and met King Hring, and the messengers asked whether the king wanted to marry this woman or send her back the way she came. The king looked well upon the woman and married her immediately. He did not give any heed to the fact that she was not from a wealthy family. The king was somewhat old, and this quickly became apparent from the way the new queen acted.

Chapter 25

A certain man lived a short way from King Hring. He had a wife and among his children there was one daughter who was named Bera. She was of a young age and beautiful. Bjorn, son of King Hring, and Bera, the farmer's daughter, played together as children, and they got along well. In his youth, the farmer was the best of fighters and had gone out raiding for long periods, and he had become a wealthy man.

Bera and Bjorn loved each other greatly, and they met frequently.

Some time passed with no news. Prince Bjorn matured greatly in the meantime, and he became both large and strong. He was well trained in all kinds of sporting competitions.

King Hring was out of the land for long periods on raids, and Hvít stayed at home and ruled the country. She was not popular among the people, but she was very pleasant and cheerful to Bjorn. He acknowledged her little. One time, when the king went from home, Queen Hvít said to King Hring that his son Bjorn ought to stay home to be with her and help her rule the land. The king thought this seemed advisable.

The queen now became arrogant and proud. The king told his son Bjorn that he must remain at home and guard the land with the queen. Bjorn said he thought little of this and that he felt very unkindly toward his stepmother the queen. The king said, however, that he must remain behind. Then the king departed the land with a great army.

Bjorn went home after this discussion with his father, at which they had disagreed so vehemently. He went to his bed and was uncheerful, and looked red as blood. The queen went to speak with him and wanted to cheer him up, and she spoke in such a way as to kindle amorous feelings in Bjorn. He told her to go away. She did so. But she often came to speak with him and said that it would be very good if they shared one bed while the king was away, and said their dealings with one another would be much better than what she had with such an old man as his father was. Bjorn heard this suggestion with disgust and slapped her hard on the face, telling her to drag herself away from him and do it quickly.

She told him she was not accustomed to being beaten or struck, "And you, Bjorn, think it's better to embrace a farmer's daughter. And that perhaps suits you, and is expected, but it is more shameful than if you enjoyed my love and good cheer. And I would not be surprised if something happens to get in the way of your stubbornness and stupidity."

She then struck him with wolfskin gloves and said that he would be turned into a savage and grim cave-bear, "And yet no food will satisfy you besides your own father's livestock. You will kill them for your meals, more than any normal bear would, and you will never get out of this curse, and this reminder will be worse for you than if you had none."

Chapter 26

Following this, Bjorn disappeared, and no one knew what had become of him. Men noticed his absence and looked for him, but they never found him, as might be expected. It might now be told that the king's livestock began to be found slaughtered in huge numbers, and a large, fearsome gray bear was blamed.

One evening it happened that Bera, the farmer's daughter, saw this fearsome bear. The bear came to her and was very cheerful with her. And she thought she recognized in this bear the eyes of Prince Bjorn, and she feared it only a little bit. The animal then went away from her, but she followed it until it came to a certain cave. And as she entered the cave, there stood a man before her and he greeted her as Bera, the farmer's daughter. She recognized that this was Bjorn, Son of Hring, and it was a reunion of great joy. They remained in the cave for a while, because she did not wish to be parted from him while there was any choice. But he told her it was not suitable for her to remain with him, for he was an animal during the day but a man during the night.

King Hring now returned home from raiding, and he was told what news had come to pass while he was away. He was told of the disappearance of his son Bjorn, and also about the great bear that had come to the land and killed livestock, mostly the king's own. The queen strongly urged the king to have the bear killed, although this was put off for a while. The king let few of his thoughts on this matter be known, and thought it was a strange situation.

One night when Bera was in bed with Prince Bjorn, Bjorn told her, "I suspect that my death-day will come tomorrow and they will kill me in the hunt. And I do not find it joyful to live with this curse that lies upon me, although I have had one single pleasure, which was my time spent together with you, though that will now be ended. I will give you this ring that I have under my left hand. You must watch the hunt, during which I will be killed, tomorrow, and when I am dead, go to the king and ask him to give you whatever is under the left shoulder of the bear. He will agree to this. The queen will have her suspicions about it, and when you intend to leave, she will give you some of the bear-meat to eat. You must not eat it, because you are pregnant, as you are aware, and you will give birth to three boys who will be my sons. And it will be visible upon them if you eat the bear-meat. This queen is the greatest of witches.

"After this, go home to your father, and there you will give birth to the boys. One will seem worst to you, however. And if you cannot manage at home on account of their bad fates and recklessness, lead them away, and come here to my cave with them. Here you will see a treasure chest with three layers. There will be runes there nearby that will tell you which boy is to have what. There are three weapons in the cave-wall, and each boy will have the weapon that is intended for him. Our son who comes first shall be named Thórir, the second Moose-Fródi, the third Bodvar, and I think it is likely that they will not be inconsequential men and that their names will be famous for a long time."

He told her of many other things, and then the bear form returned to him, and the bear went out and she followed it. And she looked around, and she saw that a great group of men was coming over the ridgeline, and many large dogs out before them. The bear now ran away from the cave and along the foot of the mountain in front of him. The dogs and the king's men came against him, and he was a hard opponent for them. He injured many men before they closed in on him, and he killed all the dogs. It came to pass that they formed a circle around him and he tried every direction inside this circle before he saw that he could not escape it. He then turned toward where the king stood, and he clutched the man who stood nearest him in his claws and tore him in half while he was still alive. Now the bear was so exhausted that he cast himself flat upon the ground, and the men ran at him quickly and killed him.

Bera saw all of this, and she went to the king and said, "My lord, will you give me whatever is under the left shoulder of the beast?" The king agreed to this, and said that whatever was under there would be a suitable gift for her. The king's men had mostly flayed the bear's skin off by this point. Bera went then and took the ring, and hid it, and no men saw what she took though afterward they sought to find out. The king asked who she was, because he did not know her. She told him something that seemed good to her, but that was other than the truth.

Chapter 27

Now the king went home, and Bera went with him. Queen Hvít was very cheerful and greeted Bera well, and asked who she might be. She answered untruthfully, as before. Now the queen had a great feast made and she had the bear's meat prepared as a feast for the joy of the people. Bera was kept in the queen's own little detached house and had no means to get away, because the queen suspected who she might be. And when the queen came to her there with a plate sooner than Bera had expected, there was bear-meat on the plate, and Hvít told Bera to enjoy it, though Bera did not want to eat it.

"It is a horrible shock," said Queen Hvít, "that you reject this offered gift that the queen herself sees fit to offer you! Eat it quickly, otherwise it will be something worse." She cut off a piece for her, and the end of this interaction was that Bera ate a piece.

Queen Hvít then cut off another piece and put it in Bera's mouth, and she swallowed only a tiny piece of it but then spat the rest out of her mouth and said she would eat no more of it, whether she was tortured or killed for doing so. Queen Hvít said, "It may be that something will come of even this much," and she laughed.

Then Bera went away, and she went home to her father. She had a difficult time finding respite during her hard pregnancy, and she told her father about everything that had changed about her situation and how it had turned out.

A little later she went into labor and gave birth to a boy, though he was somewhat unusual. He was a human in his top half, though he was a moose from his navel down. He was named Moose-Fródi.

Another boy was born, and he was called Thórir. He had dog's feet from the ankles down and he was called Thórir Dog-foot because of this. He was the handsomest of men in every other respect.

The third boy was born, and he was the handsomest of all three. He was named Bodvar, and there was no fault in his appearance. His mother loved Bodvar best.

Now all the boys grew up like grass, and when they dealt with other people they were fearsome and unfair about everything. Everyone was badly treated by them. Moose-Fródi injured many of the king's men, and killed some others.

Chapter 28

And so it continued like this for a while, until the boys were twelve years old. At this point they were so strong that none of the king's men could stand against them, and they could not play with other children.

Then Moose-Fróði said to his mother that he wanted to go away, "And I can't live around other men, because they are weaklings and get hurt as soon as I'm there." She told him he couldn't be around other men because of his brutality.

Bera now went to the cave and showed Moose-Fróði the treasure that his father had intended for him, because Bjorn had said what he intended for each to have. Moose-Fróði wanted to take more, because he had been given the least treasure of all of them, but he could not. And then he saw where there were weapons sticking out of the cave-wall. First he gripped the hilt of the sword, but it was so firmly embedded that he could not pull it out. Then he grasped the handle of the axe, but it was no looser. Moose-Fróði said, "I suspect the one who put these weapons here intended the distribution of the weapons to be like the distribution of the other gifts," and he gripped a small hilt, and that came loose for him immediately, and there followed out of the rock a short sword. He looked at the blade a while and then said, "The man who divided up these gifts was not a fair-minded one," and he stabbed this short sword at the cave wall with both hands and wanted to snap it in half, but the sword cut into the rock as far as the hand-guard and the steel rang out and did not break. Then Moose-Fróði said, "What does it matter if I carry this gift of my father's spite—it's not untrue that it can bite." After this he said farewell to his mother. Moose-Fróði now departed on a high mountain road and there he did evil deeds and killed men for their money, and he built himself a cabin and lived there.

By now King Hring had a suspicion about what sort of dark magic might be causing all of this, though he did not say anything publicly before the people and he let everything remain as calm as it had been before.

Chapter 29

A little later, Thórir Dog-foot told his mother that he wanted to go away, and she showed him the way to the cave and the treasure that was intended for him, and she told him about the weapons and asked him to take the axe, saying that this was what his father had said he intended. First he took hold of the sword-hilt, but the sword would not move. Then he took hold of the axe handle, and it came loose because it was intended for him. Then he took the treasure and went on his way, and told his mother farewell.

Thórir went first in the direction that took him to a meeting with his brother Moose-Fródi. He went into his brother's cabin and sat down in a chair and pulled his hood low over his face. A little later Moose-Fródi came home and did not look kindly at his unwelcome guest, and he drew his short sword and said:

> "The swords clang;
> this one sheds its sheath.
> The hand remembers
> the work of killing."

And then he sat down on a stump and was very savage-looking and he acted evil. And then Thórir said:

> "But I myself,
> in other places far off,
> have let my axe
> clang just as loud."

And then Thórir hid himself no longer, and his brother Moose-Fródi recognized him and asked him to take an equal share in everything he had acquired, because there was no shortage of wealth. Thórir did not want it. He stayed there for a while and then went away. Moose-Fródi directed him to Götaland and told him that the king there had recently died and asked him to go rule there. He told him of many other things, and said, "It is the law of Götaland that a great meeting is made and all the men of Götaland come there. A great chair is set up at the meeting, which two men can sit in comfortably, and the man who can fill the whole seat on his own is taken for king. And I believe that you would fill that space without a problem." After this they parted, and each spoke kindly to the other.

Now Thórir went his way until he came to the home of a certain jarl in Götaland, and the jarl greeted him well. Thórir spent the night there. Every man who saw Thórir said that he might well become king of Götaland on account of his size, and they said few men of his kind would be found there.

And when the meeting time came, it went just as Moose-Fródi had told him before. A particular chieftain was there to decide the matter truthfully. Many men sat down in this seat, but the chieftain said it suited none of them. Thórir went to the seat last, and immediately sat down in the chair. The chieftain said, "The seat is most befitting for you, and you will be appointed to this rulership." Then the men of Götaland gave Thórir the title of king and he was called King Thórir Dog-foot, and there are many sagas about him. He was popular and he waged many battles and he usually won the victory. Now he remained for a while in his kingdom.

Chapter 30

Bodvar was at home with his mother, who loved him very much. He was the most able of all men, and the handsomest as well, but he was not talkative with other men. One time he asked his mother who his father was. She told him about his death, the whole story of the event, and how he was cursed to an evil fate by his stepmother. Bodvar said, "I must repay this witch for her evil."

Then Bera told him that she had been forced by the queen to eat the bear's meat, "And now you can see it in your brothers, Thórir and Moose-Fródi."

Bodvar said, "I don't regard Moose-Fródi as any less obligated to avenge our father on this witch-hussy than he is to kill innocent men for their money and do evil deeds, and I thought it was strange that when Thórir went away, he did nothing to pay back this hag for us. The best thing for me to do, is pay her back for our trouble."

Bera said, "Be careful about this, so that she cannot affect you with her magic and harm you."

Bodvar said he would do so. After this, Bera and Bodvar went to see the king and now on Bodvar's advice Bera told the king everything, and how Bjorn's life had ended, and showed him the ring that she had taken from under the shoulder of the bear and which once Bjorn, his son, had owned. The king replied that he certainly did recognize the ring, and "I have come close to suspecting that all of this dark magic that's happened here was the work of Queen Hvít, but because of my love for her I have let all remain quiet."

Bodvar said, "Make her leave this place, otherwise we will avenge this on her."

The king said he wanted to pay Bodvar some money in compensation, whatever he himself wanted, if he would remain calm toward Hvít. He offered Bodvar lands to rule and the title of jarl, and the title of king after his own death if nothing was done to harm Queen Hvít.

Bodvar said that he had no wish to be a king, but would rather stay with the king and serve him. And then Bodvar said, "King Hring, you are such a prisoner of this monster that you barely have kept your wits about you nor even ruled righteously, and she will not live here after this."

Bodvar was so furious that the king did not dare to discuss this further with him. Now Bodvar went to Queen Hvít's little detached house and he had a certain bag with him. King Hring and Bera went after him. And when Bodvar came inside the house, he turned to Queen Hvít and put the shrunken leather bag over her head and strangled her neck from below. Then he began giving her powerful blows to the face and he beat her to death with various tortures and then dragged her body through all the streets. Many, or most, within the king's hall thought that this was not worse than half-deserved, but the king took it very badly and could think of nothing to do.

In this way Queen Hvít lost her wretched life. Bodvar was eighteen years old when this was done.

A little while later, King Hring became ill and died. After this Bodvar took over the kingdom and was content with it only a short time. Then he summoned a meeting with his people and he spoke there of his intention to depart. And he married his mother to a man named Valsleit, who had previously been a jarl, and Boðvar sat at their wedding feast, before he rode away.

Chapter 31

After this Boðvar rode away alone, and he had with him neither much gold nor silver nor other possessions, except that he was well furnished with weapons and clothes.

First he rode his good horse to the cave, according to the directions of his mother. The sword came loose when he took hold of the hilt, and this was a sword that could never be drawn unless it were to be the death of a man. It was a sword that must not be laid under a man's head nor propped up by its hilt. It could be sharpened only three times in its life, and it had this further difficulty, that it would refuse to be drawn at times. All of the brothers had wanted this mighty treasure. Boðvar made a belt out of birch for carrying the sword.

Boðvar went to visit his brother Moose-Fróði. There is nothing to tell of his journey before he came one day in the afternoon to a large cabin where Moose-Fróði was master of the house. Boðvar led his horse inside the stable, and felt that he had everything he needed right here in this cabin. Moose-Fróði came home in the evening and his eyes looked around evilly. Boðvar showed no reaction to this, and he did not rise from his seat.

The two men's horses were also getting along badly, and each tried to drive the other out of the stable. Then Moose-Fróði said, "It's a truly brave man who dares to sit down here without my permission." Boðvar pulled his hood down and said nothing. Moose-Fróði stood up and drew his short sword and stood smacking it in his palm, and then he did this a second time. Boðvar did not react. The third time, Moose-Fróði drew the short sword and advanced toward him, thinking that this man who had come had no ability to fear, but he thought he would subdue him in wrestling. Now Boðvar saw that he was coming into danger, and he waited no longer and stood up and ran straight at Moose-Fródi and gripped him below the shoulders. Moose-Fródi was a stronger grappler, and the two wrestled with many locks and holds, and then Bodvar's hood fell from his face and Moose-Fródi recognized him and said, "Welcome, kinsman, and I think we've wrestled long enough."

"No one's gotten hurt," replied Bodvar.

Moose-Fródi said, "Kinsman, you should be more careful about wrestling with me, if we try it again, because you'll notice a difference in strength if we grapple a second time and we use our full powers." Moose-Fródi offered to let Bodvar stay there with him and keep half of everything for himself. Bodvar did not want this, and he thought it was wrong to kill men for their possessions.

Now he went away, but Moose-Fródi went on the road along with him and told him that he had given many men mercy if they were small, and Bodvar cheered up when he heard this and told his brother that he did well, "And you really ought to let most of them go in peace, even if you think they're a little bit of trouble."

Moose-Fródi said, "Everything is destined to go badly for me, but for you there is one destiny and that is to go and meet King Hrólf, because all the best warriors want to be with him on account of the fact that his greatness, energy, and behavior are much better than all other kings'." Then Moose-Fródi shoved Bodvar, and he said, "You aren't as strong as you ought to be, kinsman." Then Moose-Fródi cut himself in the calf and asked Bodvar to drink, and Bodvar did so. Then Moose-Fródi shoved him a second time, and this time Bodvar stood still in his tracks. "Now you're really strong, kinsman," said Moose-Fródi, "and I expect you'll find the drink's done you good, and you will be better than everyone else in strength and energy and in all kinds of toughness and manliness, and I grant this to you happily." After this Moose-Fródi kicked a rock that was next to him with his hoof, and he said, "I will come every day to this hoofprint and see what is in it. There will be earth, if you die of sickness, water if you die at sea, and blood if you die in combat, and I will avenge you because I love you the most of all men."

Chapter 32

Now they parted, and Boðvar traveled until he came to Götaland, where King Thórir Dog-foot was not at home. Boðvar and Thórir looked so alike that no man could tell one from the other, and the men of Götaland assumed that Thórir had come home. Boðvar was shown to "his" throne, and in all respects he was served just as if he had been the king and placed in bed alongside the queen, because Thórir was now married. Boðvar did not wish to lie under her blanket, and she thought this was strange because she believed this was truly her husband, but Boðvar told her everything about how the situation was. She did not allow anyone to see any sign of it on her face. And in this way they spent each night speaking with each other, until Thórir came home, and then men realized who this man was. There was a joyful reunion of the two brothers, and Thórir said he would have trusted no other man to sleep so near to his queen. Thórir offered to let Boðvar stay there and take half of his movable property as his own, but Boðvar said he did not want that. Then Thórir offered to go with him if he wanted, or to get him a following of men. Boðvar did not want this either. Then Boðvar rode away, and Thórir went with him down the road for a while, and the two brothers parted in friendship and yet with a certain secret. And nothing is told of Boðvar's journey before he came to Denmark and was a short way from Lejre.

Chapter 33

One day there was a severe downpour, and Boðvar became very wet. The horse became exhausted and began to falter under him when he rode a great deal, and became very soggy and worn out. Deep darkness began to descend, and a harder rain during the night. And Boðvar noticed nothing until his horse struck his front hooves on something in front of him.

Boðvar dismounted and looked, and saw that there must be some house there, and then he found the door, which he knocked on. A man came outside, and Boðvar asked him for lodging during that night. The man of the house said that he wouldn't turn him away in the middle of the night even though he was a stranger. He thought this visitor seemed like a hulking man, from what he could see of him. Bodvar stayed there that night in good hospitality. He asked many questions about King Hrólf's great deeds and those of his champions, and whether it might be a long trip to there.

"No," said the farmer, "It's a very short journey there. Do you intend to go there?"

"Yes," said Bodvar. "That is my intention."

The farmer told him that would be very suitable, "Because I see that you are a big, strong man, and they all think of themselves as real tough guys."

And when they spoke of King Hrólf and his champions, the farmer's wife began to weep in a loud voice. "Why do you weep, old woman?" asked Bodvar.

She said, "My husband and I had one son, who was named Hott. And when he went to town one day to amuse himself, the king's men made fun of him and he reacted unhappily. Then they took him and put him in a pile of cast-off bones, and it is their habit during mealtimes to throw every bone at him, once they have finished eating all the meat off it. Sometimes he gets hurt badly from this, if a bone hits him, and I don't know whether he's alive or dead. And I want to ask this favor from you in return for my hospitality, that you throw only small bones and not big ones at him, if he isn't already dead."

Bodvar said, "I will do as you ask, and I don't think it's manly to beat people with bones or to hate children or small people."

"Then you do well," said the woman, "because your hand looks strong to me, and I know that he couldn't withstand your blows if you didn't restrain yourself."

Chapter 34

Then Bodvar made his way to Lejre, and he came to the king's hall. He led his horse inside the stable next to the king's best horses without asking anyone about it, and then he went into the hall where there were few people present. He sat toward the outside, and after he had been there a little while, he heard a rustling noise in a certain corner. Bodvar looked that way and saw a human hand come up out of a big pile of bones lying there. The hand was very dirty.

Bodvar went over, and asked who was in the pile of bones.

He was answered, and not in a courageous voice: "My name is Hott, friendly fellow."

"Why are you here," said Bodvar, "and what are you doing?"

Hott said, "I'm making myself a shield-wall, friendly fellow."

Bodvar said, "You've got a poor one."

Bodvar reached for him and plucked him out from the pile of bones. Hott screamed out loud in response and said, "Now you're going to kill me! Don't do it! I've done so much work on it already, and now you've broken up my shield-wall, and I had just now made it high enough that it protected me against all your assaults, so that no bone had hit me for a long time. But it still wasn't as complete as it ought to have been."

Bodvar said, "You won't be able to work on your shield-wall any longer."

Hott began to cry and said, "Are you going to kill me now, fellow?"

Bodvar told him to hush up, and picked him up and took him outside the hall to some water that was nearby and washed him all over. There were few people in the vicinity who paid any attention. Then Bodvar went back to the seat on the bench that he had taken earlier, and he brought Hott with him and set Hott there next to him. Hott was so afraid that he was trembling in every limb. But he seemed to understand that this man wanted to help him.

After the evening came and men began to file into the hall, Hrólf's champions saw that Hott was sitting up on a bench. They thought the man who had done this had a share of courage. Hott had an ominous look on his face when he saw these men he recognized, because he had experienced only evil at their hands. He wanted badly to go back into his pile of bones and live, but Bodvar held on to him so that he could not go away. Hott thought that he wouldn't be as vulnerable to the thrown bones if he got there, as he would be where he was now.

The warriors kept up their usual habit and threw bones across the hall at Bodvar and Hott, small bones at first. Bodvar acted as if he did not see this. Hott was so terrified that he neither took food nor drink, and he thought he would be struck at any moment. He said to Boðvar, "Friendly fellow, there's a big piece of bone coming your way, and it's intended to cause us real harm." Boðvar told him to shut up. Boðvar held up an open palm and caught the bone in this way, and it was the bones of a whole leg. Boðvar threw it back, aiming at the man who threw it, and he threw it at him so straight and hard that he killed him. Then a great fear came over the king's warriors.

Now the news came to King Hrólf and his champions up in the castle, that an imposing man had come to the hall and killed one of his warriors, and the men wanted to kill this man. King Hrólf asked whether this warrior of his had been killed without cause. "Nearly so," they said.

And now when all of the truth about this was revealed to King Hrólf, the king said that he was far from thinking Boðvar ought to be killed. "You have taken up a bad habit here of beating innocent men with bones. There is dishonor for me, and shame for you, in doing this. I have always said this about it in the past, and you have given it no heed. I think this man you have accused must be very far from inconsequential. Summon him to me that I might know who he is."

Boðvar went before the king and greeted him courteously. The king asked him for his name. "Your warriors call me 'Hott's lackey,' but my name is Boðvar."

The king said, "What repayment will you offer me for my warrior?" Boðvar said, "He dealt out the same as he got."

The king said, "Do you want to be my man and take over his seat?"

"I won't refuse to be your man, but Hott and I won't part in that case. And we will both take seats nearer to you than this man sat, otherwise we will both depart."

The king said, "I see no honor in him, but I won't grudge him food."

Now Boðvar went to the seat that he pleased, as he did not want the one the other man had. He displaced three men with the room he needed to sit, and then Hott and he sat down there within the hall in better seats than they had been assigned. Men did not enjoy dealing with Boðvar, and they had great hate of him.

Chapter 35

As it neared Yule, the men became uncheerful, and Bodvar asked Hott what this was about. Hott told him that a large and terrifying beast had come there two winters in a row. "It has wings on its back, and it is always flying. For two autumns now it has been coming and doing terrible harm. No weapons bite it, and even the champions of the king who are greatest of all never come home after meeting it."

Bodvar said, "This hall here isn't as well managed as I thought, if one animal can destroy the kingdom and the property of the king."

Hott said, "It isn't an animal, but more like the greatest troll."

Now it came to Yule Eve, and the king said, "I want you men to be calm and quiet tonight, and I ban all of my men from getting into danger with the creature—but as for the cattle, it will go as fate wills. I don't want to lose my men." All the men gave the king their promise about this.

Bodvar hid himself at some distance away during the night. He made Hott come with him. Hott did this unwillingly, and said he was being steered into his death. Bodvar said it would go better than that. They walked away from the hall, and Hott became so afraid that Bodvar had to carry him. Now they saw the animal, and Hott immediately screamed as loudly as he could and said the creature was going to swallow him. Bodvar called him a cur and told him to be silent, and threw him down into the moss where he lay not at all unafraid, and did not dare to go home either. Now Bodvar faced the creature, but it so happened that his sword was lodged firmly in his sword-belt, and now he drew off the sword-belt, so that the sword came out of its sheath, and he immediately put it under the beast's shoulder so hard that it hit the heart, and then the beast dropped dead to the ground.

After this Bodvar went to where Hott was lying, and then picked him up and took him to where the dead animal lay. Hott shivered uncontrollably. Bodvar said, "Now you will drink the blood of the beast." Hott was reluctant for a long while, but of course he dared to do nothing else. Bodvar made him drink two large gulps, and then he made him eat a little of the beast's heart. Then Bodvar grappled him, and the two wrestled a long time, after which Bodvar said, "You have certainly become strong, and I don't expect that you'll fear the warriors of King Hrólf now."

Hott said, "I won't fear them, and I won't fear you, after this."

"Then that's well done, Hott my companion. Now let's go and pick up the creature and prepare it in such a way that others will think it is alive." They did so, and after this they went home and were quiet, and no one knew what they had accomplished.

Chapter 36

In the morning the king asked what the men knew about the beast, and whether it had visited them at all during the night. He was told that all the livestock animals were doing well inside their pens and were uninjured. The king told men to investigate whether anyone had seen a sign that the creature had come there. The watchmen went out to do so, and they came back soon after and told the king that the animal was on the move, and dangerously close to the town. The king told his men to be brave and told every man to be as much use as he had courage for, and to kill this monster. And it was done as the king commanded, and they prepared themselves for this.

Then the king looked at the animal and said, "I don't see that it's moving at all. Who wants to earn a reward and go against it?"

Bodvar said, "That would certainly be a prize for a bold man. Hott my companion, take this chance now to get rid of your bad reputation, since men say there is no spirit and no good in you. Go now, and kill the beast. You can see that none of the others are eager to do this."

"Yes," said Hott, "I will do this."

The king said, "I don't know where this boldness in you comes from, Hott, and a great deal has changed about you in a short while."

Hott said, "Give me the sword Gullinhjalti, which you are holding, and then I will kill the creature or die."

King Hrólf said, "This sword cannot be held except by a man who is virtuous and a brave warrior."

Hott said, "You will see that I have those properties."

The king said, "Who knows, maybe more has changed about your behavior than meets the eye. But only vanishingly few observers would recognize you as the same man. Now, take the sword and be most fortunate in using it, if this is well done."

Then Hott went at the creature very daringly and struck it when he came into reach, and the beast fell down dead.

Bodvar said, "You see now, lord, what he has done."

The king said, "He has certainly changed a great deal, but Hott has not killed the animal alone. It was you instead who did that."

Bodvar said, "It may be that it is so."

The king said, "I knew when you came here that few men would be equal to you. But I think that your greatest deed is that you made me another champion from Hott, who seemed unlikely to win much good fortune. And now I don't want him to be named Hott any longer. He will be named Hjalti from now on, after the sword Gullinhjalti."

And here ends the tale of Bodvar and his brothers.

Part 5: The Tale of Hjalti

Chapter 37

Now the winter passed, until it was nearly time for King Hrólf's berserkers to come home. Bodvar asked Hjalti about the habits of the berserkers, and Hjalti told him that it was their habit, when they came home to the hall, to walk up to every man and ask him if he thought he was a match for them. And first of all they would ask this of the king.

But then the king would say, "It would be difficult to say, such equally manly men as you are, when you have made yourselves famous in battles and bloodshed against various peoples in the southern half of the world as well as in the northern," and the king would answer in this way more from courtesy than humility, because he knew their state of mind, and because they had won him great victories and great wealth.

Then the berserkers would leave that man and go and ask the same of each man who was in the hall, and none would say he was a match for them.

Bodvar said, "There aren't many real men here, if they all let the berserkers call them such cowards." Then they ended this conversation.

Bodvar had now been with King Hrólf for one year. And now the next Yule Eve came, and one moment King Hrólf was sitting at his table when the doors to his hall sprang open, and twelve berserkers strolled in. They were so gray with all the iron arms and armor they wore, that looking at them was like looking at shattered ice.

Bodvar whispered to Hjalti and asked him whether he'd dare to test himself against one of these berserkers. "Yes," said Hjalti, "and not just against one. Against them all—because I don't know how to feel fear, not even if all their numbers are brought against me alone. One of them won't make me tremble."

Now the berserkers came into the hall, and they saw that King Hrólf's champions had multiplied since they had left. They looked carefully at the newcomers, and thought that one of them certainly wasn't little, and the one who walked first wasn't a little surprised at that. Now, as they were accustomed to do, they came before King Hrólf and asked him the same question in the same words as they usually did. And the king answered as he usually did, and then they went before each man in the hall. And the last men they approached were the two companions. The first one asked Bodvar whether he thought he was an even match for him. Bodvar said he didn't think he was an even match, he thought he was even more of a man than the berserker—no matter what the test was. And, Bodvar added, this foul son of a mare in front of him didn't need to prattle on about it like these other geldings. And with this said, Bodvar shot forward at the berserker and got a hold on him from beneath (though he was in all his armor), and drove him down to the floor in a heavy fall, so that the berserker lay as if all his bones were broken.

For his part, Hjalti did much the same to another berserker. Then there was a terrible noise in the hall, and King Hrólf decided he was watching a dangerous portent if his own men were murdering each other. He leapt off of his throne, toward Bodvar, and told him to be at ease and in good form. But Bodvar replied that the berserker would die, unless he said he was a lesser man. King Hrólf said it was easily done, and he had the berserker stand up, and Hjalti also did as the king instructed.

Then the men sat down, each one in his own seat, and the berserkers sat down in their own seats with great irritation. King Hrólf told them many stories, so that they could see that nothing was so great, or so strong, or so large that its equal could not be found. "So I forbid you to start any kind of trouble in my hall, and if you break this law, it will cost your life. But be as cruel as you like when I have need of you to fight my enemies—and you'll win yourselves honor and glory. I have such a great selection of warriors here that I have no need to rely on you berserkers alone."

Everyone received the king's words well, and so they reconciled with whole hearts. The hall was now arranged in such a way that Boðvar was considered and treated as the greatest, and he sat up by the king's right hand. And next to him was Hjalti the Righteous, a name that the king had given him. He was called "the Righteous" because he went every day with the king's bodyguards, who had treated him in the way told of before, and he never did them any harm even though he had now become a greater man than they were. And yet the king would have forgiven him, if he had given them something to remember that bad treatment by, or had killed one of them.

And at the king's left hand sat the three brothers, Svipdag, Hvítserk, and Beigað, as they had become men of great repute. And next were the twelve berserkers, and then the best of the warriors on both sides down the length of the hall, men who are not named here. The king let his men carry on with all sorts of games and tests of skill, with joy and good fun for all involved. And it was Boðvar who tested himself the most of all his champions, whatever the test might be, and he came to be regarded so highly by King Hrólf that he was married to Drífa, the king's only daughter.

And now some time passed, and they sat in their kingdom, and they were the most famous of all men.

Part 6: Concerning Adils, King at Uppsala, and King Hrólf's Journey to Sweden with His Champions

Chapter 38

It is said that one day King Hrólf sat in his royal hall with all his champions and his best men with him, and he held a grand feast.

At one point King Hrólf looked all around him and said, "A spectacular force of men is gathered here into one hall." Then Hrólf asked Bodvar if he knew any other king like himself, any who had such champions. Bodvar said he lacked one thing. The king asked what.

Bodvar answered, "What you're still lacking, my lord, is that you haven't claimed your inheritance from your father in Uppsala, where your in-law King Adils unjustly holds it."

King Hrólf said that it would be difficult to recover it, "Because King Adils is not a simple man, but a sorcerer—and deceitful, and tricky, and clever, and cruel, and the hardest sort of man to fight."

Bodvar said, "But it would befit you, my lord, to recover what's yours and meet with King Adils one time, to know how he might respond to this matter."

King Hrólf said, "This is a serious matter that you bring up, because I also need to see about avenging my father, where the greedy and treacherous King Adils is. I will dare it."

"I will not speak ill of you for it," replied Bodvar. "If you try for what's yours, whatever might be in store where King Adils awaits."

Chapter 39

Now King Hrólf prepared for his journey with a hundred men, in addition to his twelve champions and twelve berserkers. Nothing is said of their journey before they came to the home of a certain wealthy farmer. The farmer stood outside when they arrived, and invited them all to stay there.

King Hrólf said, "You are a good man! But do you have the capacity for it? We are not few in number, and we could not all be hosted on one small farm."

The farmer laughed and said, "Yes, my lord. I have seen men no fewer in number come here, and you will not lack for drink or anything you might need the whole night long."

The king said, "Then we'll chance it."

The farmer was glad at this. Their horses were now taken away, and the men were hospitably treated. The place was so accommodating, the men didn't think they'd ever been in a more welcoming place. The farmer was extremely cheerful, and the men could not ask him any question that he could not answer in some way, and they thought he was the least stupid of all men.

Sleep now took them. And when they woke, it was so cold that the teeth shook in their skulls. They all struggled up and threw all the clothes and every kind of covering they could reach on themselves—except King Hrólf's twelve champions, who got by with just the clothes they had on them from before. All of them were cold throughout the night.

In the morning the farmer asked, "How have you fellows slept?"

"Well," Bodvar said.

Then the farmer said to Hrólf, "Your men found it a little cool here in the hall at night, and it was. But they cannot imagine that they can withstand the difficulties that King Adils will test them with at Uppsala, if they thought this was so difficult. Send half your army home, my lord, if you want to keep your life. It won't be by superior numbers that you defeat King Adils."

"You are an exceptional man, farmer," said Hrólf, "and I will take the advice you offer."

Now they kept to the road which they had planned to take, and they told the farmer farewell. The king sent home half of his army.

Now they kept riding down the road, and soon another small farm appeared before them. Here they thought they recognized the same farmer who had hosted them the night before. They suspected something unusual might be happening.

This farmer greeted them well, and asked them why they came so often. The king said, "We certainly don't know what kind of magic tricks are getting played on us, but you must be called a true magician."

The farmer said, "All the same, I can't greet you less well this time." So they spent another night in good comfort. Sleep fell on them, but then they awoke with such a great thirst upon them that they found it nearly unbearable, and could barely move the tongues in their mouths. They stood up and went to where there was a large keg of wine, and they drank straight from it.

In the morning, the farmer, whose name was Hrani, said "I hope it is still true, my lord, that you will heed me. I think there is little grit in the men who had to take a drink during the night. They will have to put up with harder challenges when you visit King Aðils."

And then a great storm struck up, and they stayed at this farm over the next day. The third night came, and a fire was made for them. It was very hot for those who sat near it. Most of them rushed out of the room that Hrani had given them, and they all got far away from the fire except King Hrólf and his champions.

Hrani said, "My lord, you must choose men from out of your army. It is my advice that you go on with only yourself and your twelve champions. Then there is some hope that you will come back, but none otherwise."

"It looks to me, farmer," said King Hrólf, "as if I'll take your advice." They had been there three nights, and then the king rode on with the twelve men, and sent all the rest of his troops back.

King Aðils heard about this and said it was good that King Hrólf wanted to visit him at home, "Because he certainly has business here, and it will be worth a story before we part."

Chapter 40

After this, King Hrólf and his champions rode to the hall of King Aðils. All the common people of that place crowded into the highest towers of the city to look upon the glory of King Hrólf and his champions, because they were dressed in the finest clothes, and many thought that such noble riders were a very worthy sight. At first they rode slowly and with magnificent grace, but when they had only a short way left to the hall, they struck their horses with their spurs and ran them toward the hall, so that everyone that stood before them shrank away in retreat.

King Adils ordered them to be greeted with eager joy, and offered to have their horses seen to.

Bodvar said, in response to this: "See to it, stable-boys, that not a single hair from the forelock, or the tail, gets out of its place. And watch them well and thoughtfully, so that not a speck of dirt touches them."

King Adils was told how assiduously they had spoken about the care of their horses. Adils said, "They show tremendous pride and insolence. Now listen to my words, and do as I say: Cut off their horses' tails down to the bone, down where they grow from, near the anus. And cut off their forelocks down to the skin, and treat their horses as mockingly as possible in everything you do, and do everything else wicked short of killing them."

Now Hrólf and his men were led to the doors of the hall, but not where they could see King Adils as yet. Svipdag said, "They know me here from before, so I will walk in first because I have the clearest idea about what might be done to us, or what they might have prepared for us. Say not a word that suggests who King Hrólf is, so that King Adils will not be able to know him from any other man in our group." Then Svipdag walked in ahead of all of them, then his brothers Hvítserk and Beigad after him, then King Hrólf and Bodvar, and then each of the rest of them in turn. No servants were there, since they had left after they had invited the Danes into the hall.

The champions had their hawks on their shoulders, which was considered a very proud thing to do in those times. King Hrólf himself had his hawk named Hábrók.

Svipdag continued to advance forward, and he looked carefully in all directions. He saw that much had changed in every part of the hall. They walked over several hindrances that had been placed there for them, and which it is not possible to describe. These became harder, as they progressed farther into the hall.

And now they came far enough into the hall that they saw where King Adils sat puffed up in his throne. It seemed to the men in both parties that this was a momentous occasion. Then they saw that the only easy path forward brought them before King Adils, and by now they had come so near him and his men that they could make out each other's speech.

Then King Adils spoke: "And you also have come here, my old companion Svipdag! What is this champion's errand? Could it not be, as it seems to me, that

"The arrow's in the neck,
the eye's left the head,
the scar's in the brow,
and two cuts in the hand?

"And Beigad, your brother, is weakened all over."

Svipdag spoke with such a loud voice that all could hear, "Now I want to receive mercy from you, King Adils. And in accordance with what our understanding once was, I want peace for all twelve of us men here."

King Adils said, "I will agree to this. Come into the hall swiftly and boldly, with a trusting heart."

It seemed to them that trenches had been dug all around the hall on the inside of its walls, but testing what was there would not be cheaply done. And there was so much darkness over King Adils that they could not see his face clearly. They also saw that the tapestries that were set up around the hall to adorn it, were let down in certain places, and they thought there were likely men with weapons behind them.

True to their suspicions, when the champions crossed over the trenches, an armored man rushed out from under each fold. King Hrólf and his champions put up a hard defense and chopped through their skulls down to the teeth.

For a while it continued like this, and the Swedes did not recognize which of them was King Hrólf, while they were falling down like pouring water.

Now King Adils swelled with anger in his throne, when he saw that King Hrólf's champions broke down his troops as though they were so many dogs. And when he saw that the attack could not succeed, he stood up and said, "Who stands to gain from all this noise? You are terrible criminals, you men who are attacking King Hrólf and his champions, who have visited us here at home! Stop this immediately and sit down! Now Hrólf, my in-law, let us be together in joy, all of us."

Svipdag said, "You don't hold the peace well, King Aðils, and you are honorless in your words." But they sat down after this, with Svipdag nearest King Aðils, and then Hjalti the Righteous, and then Boðvar and King Hrólf, because they did not want him to be recognized.

King Aðils said, "I see that you don't seek the respect of men in an unknown land. Why does Hrólf my in-law not have more men?"

Svipdag said, "I see that you don't hesitate to connive against King Hrólf and his men, and it's a wonder he comes here at all—with few or with many." And so their conversation ended.

Chapter 41

After that, King Aðils ordered the hall cleared out. The dead were carried away—and many of King Aðils's men had been killed and a great many more injured. King Aðils said, "Let's now start the fires in the center of the hall for our friends, and let's serve these men seriously, so that all of us are well pleased." Men were now sent to kindle fires for them. Hrólf's champions sat with their weapons always at hand, and would not let go of them. The fire got going quickly, because there was no shortage of pitch and dry wood thrown in. King Aðils set himself and his elite bodyguards up on the other side of the fire from King Hrólf and his champions, and each side sat on long benches and spoke quite a bit among themselves.

King Aðils said, "It is no exaggeration what they say about your courage and toughness, Hrólf's champions, and you think yourselves greater than all others. It is no lie what they say about your strength. Now stoke the fire, because I cannot tell which is the king, and I know that you will not flee the fire, though you might get a little warm." It was done as he ordered, and he wanted to be sure where King Hrólf was, because he thought that he would not be able to stand the heat as well as his champions, and he thought that it would be easier to seize him if he knew where he was, because he truly wanted King Hrólf dead. Boðvar understood this, as did some of the others, and they shielded him somewhat from the heat, as well as they could, but not so well that he would be easily picked out.

And when the fire was at its hottest, King Hrólf remembered what he had previously vowed, to flee neither fire nor iron. And he saw now that King Aðils wanted to make a test of this vow, by forcing them either to burn there or fail to heed the vow.

Then they saw that King Aðils's throne had been carried out of the hall, and so had his men's seats. Now the fire was burning through its fuel and was reaching an intense pitch, and they saw that the flames would touch them if they did nothing. Now their clothes were mostly burned away, and they threw their shields on the fire.

Boðvar and Svipdag said,

> "Let's stoke these fires
> in Aðils's city."

Then each champion grabbed some of the men who were stoking the fire, and flung them into the flames and said, "Now enjoy this warmth as payment for your work and trouble, because we're fully warmed up. Now you warm up, because you were so hard-working for a while when it came to warming us." Hjalti grabbed a third man and flung him into the flames at his end of the fire, and did the same to all the rest of the men. There they burned to ash, and no one came to save them because all feared to get so close the flames. After this was done, King Hrólf said,

> "The man who leaps the fire
> is not a coward who flees it."

And then they all flung themselves over the flames and intended to grab King Aðils. When King Aðils saw this, he elected to save himself and ran to a tree that stood in the hall with a hollow inside of it, and thus he escaped the hall with his sorcery and magic spells. From there he came into the hall of Queen Yrsa, where he found her talking. She greeted him roughly and spoke many harsh words to him. "First you had my husband, King Helgi, killed," she said, "and treated him shamefully and kept property from the one who rightfully owned it, and now, with that behind you, you want to kill my son. You are a man much worse and much crueler than any other. Now I will do everything in my power to see that King Hrólf gets his property, and you will receive only dishonor, as you deserve."

Adils said, "Then it will go that way, and we won't trust each other. From now on, I will not come within their sight." And now their talk was ended.

Chapter 42

Then Queen Yrsa went to meet King Hrólf and she greeted him very well. He also received her greeting well. She summoned a man named Vogg to serve them properly. And when this man came before King Hrólf, Vogg said, "This man is thin and his face looks like a pole-ladder [*kraki*]. Is this really your king?"

King Hrólf said, "You've given me a name that will stick. What do you give me as a naming-gift?"

Vogg answered, "Everything I have, because I'm penniless."

The king said, "Then the one who does have something must give to the other." So he took a golden ring from his hand and gave it to this man.

Vogg said, "Be the healthiest of all men for your gift! This is the greatest of all treasures!"

And when the king saw the man valued it so much, he said, "It doesn't take much to please Vogg."

Vogg stood up with one foot on a stump and said, "I swear this oath, that I will avenge you if you are killed by men's hands and I outlive you."

The king said, "There are perhaps men more likely to accomplish that than you, but good will come of you, Vogg."

They understood that this man would be faithful and true, as far as that went with the little he could do. And though they thought that he couldn't be counted on to do much, because he seemed like a worthless man, they hid nothing from him.

Now they intended to sleep, and they thought that they would be able to rest unafraid in the rooms that the queen gave them. Boðvar said, "Everything is suitably prepared for us here, and the queen wishes us well even if King Aðils wishes us all the evil he can. It would be well done for us to accept this offering."

Vogg told them that King Aðils was a great maker of sacrifices, "Such as has no peer. He sacrifices to a boar, and I doubt that any other enemy so formidable exists. Be watchful of yourselves, because he is putting his every thought and resource into overcoming you in any way possible."

"I think it's more likely," said Boðvar, "that he is thinking about the way he fled his own hall from us this evening."

Vogg said, "But remember also that he will be deceptive and cruel."

Chapter 43

They went to sleep after this, but awoke when they heard a noise outside that was so loud that the house they lay in seemed to tremble, as if someone huge were batting it around. Vogg said, "The boar must have been released. King Aðils must have sent it to get his vengeance on you, and it is such a terrible troll that no one can withstand it!"

King Hrólf had a large dog named Gram who was with him. He was a large dog, and very strong.

Now this troll in a boar's shape appeared, and made a terrible noise. Boðvar sicced the dog on the boar, and the dog showed no fear but ran immediately at the boar. There was now a hard-fought battle, and Boðvar assisted the dog by swinging his weapon at the boar, though the blade would not bite the animal's back.

This dog Gram was so mighty that he ripped the ears off the boar's face and all the boar's cheeks with them, and all of a sudden the boar disappeared down into the earth just as it had come.

Then King Adils arrived with a large following, and set the house on fire. When this occurred, King Hrólf and his men realized that there was no shortage of fuel for the flames. Bodvar said, "It's a bad day for us to die, if we're going to burn in here, and it would be a bad end for King Hrólf, if it ended this way. I'd choose instead to be killed by weapons on an open battlefield. I see no better course of action for us than to rush so hard at the walls that we break out of the house, if it can be done—and that will be no child's play, since the house is strongly built. Then let each man fight the one in front of him, when he comes outside, and then the Swedes will fall back shortly."

"This is excellent advice," said King Hrólf, "and this will avail us well."

Chapter 44

Now they all made the decision together to leap at one corner of the roof with such explosive force that it was foolhardy, and at last the walls of the burning house burst asunder before them, and King Hrólf and his comrades made their escape.

By this point the streets were crowded all around with armored men, and now began the most desperate kind of battle. King Hrólf and his comrades went forward with hate in their hearts, and where they stepped it was as though the field of enemy bodies had been plowed under. There was no man among their enemies so proud or so noble that he was not made to cower in his apprehension of their sword-blows.

Down into this storm of battle flew King Hrólf's hawk, Hábrók, launching from a windowsill on the tower to settle on King Hrólf's shoulders peacefully as though the hawk had all but the assurance of victory.

Bodvar said, "That hawk acts like he's pulled off something heroic himself!" Little did they know that just then, one of the Swedes had rushed to his own king's hawk-tower and found to his bewilderment that King Hrólf's hawk had flown away, and all of King Adils's hawks were slain.

No one could withstand King Hrólf and his champions, and now the battle ended with the killing of many men. But at this time King Adils was nowhere to be seen, and no one could say what had become of him. The few Swedes who survived from among King Adils's men, begged for peace and were spared.

Now King Hrólf and his comrades went to the hall, and marched into it boldly. Bodvar asked on what bench King Hrólf would like to sit.

King Hrólf answered him, "I'll sit on the king's throne itself, and never one seat lower." King Adils never entered the hall, and they thought it was a burden to wait for him without receiving any hospitality, given how much they had done that day. But for a while they sat in peace and contentment, until Hjalti the Righteous spoke up.

"Wouldn't it be a good idea," he asked, "for someone to check up on our horses and find out if they're missing anything they need?" And someone went to do as he said, and when the man came back from checking on them, he said the horses were being treated with villainous mockery, and he gave an account then of how their horses were being mistreated, as has been told. King Hrólf showed no sign that he had even heard, but he did remark that everything seemed to be heading in only one direction for the king named Adils.

Now Queen Yrsa entered the hall and went before her son King Hrólf and greeted him in the artful and proper manner. He received this well, and she continued: "It is not as good a reunion as I'd hoped, kinsman, or as good as it ought to have been. But my son, you must not endure the inhospitality around here any longer, because there is a large army being prepared from all across Sweden, and King Adils intends to use it to kill you and all your men. That is something he has meant to do for a long time, if only it had been doable, and I believe now that your strength is greater than his witchcraft.

"And now, take this silver drinking-horn that I present to you. Inside it I have stowed all of King Adils's best rings, including the one called Sviagrís that he thinks better of than of all others." And with this horn she also gave him a great treasure in gold and silver. All of the money and treasure was so much together that hardly any one man could have held it.

Now Vogg was seen to, and he received a great quantity of gold from King Hrólf for his exceptional service. The queen ordered men to lead twelve horses forward, all of them roans except for one stallion who was white as snow, and she asked King Hrólf to ride them. Of all Aðils's armored war horses, these were the best. Yrsa gave them shields and helmets and coats of chainmail, all of them the highest quality and workmanship, because the fire had destroyed so much of their own weapons and clothing. All of these necessities that she gave them were precious.

King Hrólf said, "Have you now given me the same amount of money that I rightfully was supposed to own and that my father owned?"

She answered, "This is in fact many times more than what you were strictly owed, and in this place you and your men have won yourselves great fame. Now get ready as best you can, because you still have trials up ahead of you."

Now they mounted up on their horses. King Hrólf spoke lovingly to his mother, and they parted in joy.

Chapter 45

Now King Hrólf and his comrades rode the way down from Uppsala and vicinity, and in the place that is called Fýrisvellir it is said that King Hrólf saw a large golden ring glowing in the street before them, and this ring clanged loudly as the men rode over it.

"The ring is clanging so loudly," said King Hrólf, "because it is ill content in its loneliness." And with that, he let one of his own gold rings fall to the street as well.

He then said, "It must be told far and wide that I do not stoop to pick up gold even if it is lying on the street in front of me. And let none of my champions be so bold that he picks it up! That ring was thrown there to deter us on our journey." And they promised him this, and at that moment they also heard the sound of trumpets from every direction around them, and an enormous following army came into view. This army was moving swiftly; in fact it seemed that each man in it seemed to be letting his horse run as fast as it could.

Just the same, King Hrólf and his men rode straight on forward. Boðvar said, "These men are coming after us hard, and I certainly hope that some of them get what they want from their errand. They want to catch up with us."

The king said, "We ought to pay no attention to them. They're the ones who'll be slowing down." Now he reached down with his hand for the horn that had the gold in it, the one that Beigaðheld in his hand as he rode. And then he began to strew the gold all over the street as they rode over Fýrisvellir, until the streets glowed like gold pieces.

And when the pursuing army saw all the gold gleaming in the street, most of them leapt off their horses, thinking that whoever was quickest to start picking up gold would be the luckiest. There was a great deal of petty stealing and childish wrestling, and the one who was strongest was the one who got the most.

Because of this, the pursuing army was delayed. When King Aðils saw what was happening, he nearly lost his mind with rage, and he berated them with stinging words, saying that they were snatching up the smaller prize while they were letting the bigger prize get away, and that their foul shame would be told of soon in every land—"The fact that you let twelve men escape from us here, you, this uncountable army that I have taken pains to assemble from every region of Sweden." King Aðils then rode swiftly ahead of them all, full of rage, and now along with him came his army.

King Hrólf now saw King Aðils galloping hard and closing the distance with him, and in this moment Hrólf took the ring Svíagrís and cast it on the street before him. When Aðils saw this ring, he said, "The Swede who gave Hrólf this ring has been truer to Hrólf than to me. And yet Hrólf was given this treasure, and no sooner will I get it back." And with these words he aimed the tip of his spearshaft at the spot where the ring lay, wanting to seize it before any other man could. He bent down very far in the process as he stuck the end of the spear into the loop of the ring.

As King Hrólf saw this, he turned his own horse back and said, "I made the greatest man among the Swedes poke around like a pig." And just as King Aðils was starting to swing the tip of the spear back around to himself, Hrólf rode past him at a fast pace and chopped off both of his buttocks all the way down to the bone with his sword Skofnung, the best sword that has ever been carried in the Northlands. Hrólf told Adils to remember this shame for a little while, "And now you'll recognize King Hrólf, the one you've been seeking for such a long time, wherever I may be."

King Adils suffered great blood loss from this, so much so that he began quickly to lose his strength. He was forced now to retreat in worse shape than he'd started out, and King Hrólf retrieved the ring Svíagrís, with this having been the end of their encounter. It has never been told that the two kings met again.

And the Danes slaughtered all the men who had ridden forward far enough and risked the most—those men did not have long to wait before they met King Hrólf and his champions. And none of the champions thought he was too good to kill a Swede, and they spared none of their strength when the opportunity to kill one presented itself.

Chapter 46

Now King Hrólf and his men went riding along on their way, and they rode nearly the whole day through. As night began to fall, they came within sight of a farm and came up to the doors. There before them was the farmer Hrani, and he offered them every kind of entertainment and said that their journey hadn't gone much different than he'd predicted it would. The king said that was true, and that Hrani certainly wasn't smoke-blind.

"Here are some weapons that I want to give you," said Hrani.

King Hrólf said, "These are bizarre weapons, commoner." They were a shield, a sword, and a suit of chainmail. King Hrólf did not want the weapons.

Hrani began to get angry about this, and felt that he was being humiliated. "You aren't as well suited for these, King Hrólf," he said, "as you think you are. And you aren't always as wise as you think you are." Hrani said this refusal was disgraceful, and now he offered them no hospitality for the night.

King Hrólf and his companions wanted to ride on, though the night was dark. Hrani's eye was unsmiling, and they doubted he would offer them much beer when they refused his gifts. And Hrani did nothing to stop them from riding away as they liked, so they rode away after all this with no farewells said on either side.

Before they had been gone long, Bodvar stopped in his tracks and said, "Good ideas often occur to the unwise in hindsight. And now that is true for me; I suspect that we have not behaved entirely wisely in rejecting his gifts. We ought to have accepted them. And since we did otherwise, we might have rejected our own victory."

King Hrólf said, "I suspect the same. This man must have been Óðin the old, as he certainly was one-eyed."

"So let's ride back as fast as we can," said Svipdag, "and find out."

Now they rode back, but they found both the farm and the farmer gone. "It'll do us no good to search for him," said King Hrólf, "because he is an evil spirit." So they rode on their way, and nothing is told of their journey before they returned to their own kingdom in Denmark, and remained there in peace.

Bodvar advised King Hrólf that he participate in fewer battles from here on out. If he did so and remained quiet, his enemies would think it less likely that there was anything to gain by attacking him. But Bodvar confessed that he was unsure about how victorious the king would be in the future, if he tested his luck too much.

King Hrólf said, "Fate determines each man's destiny—not that evil spirit."

Bodvar answered, "You are the last man we want to lose, but I have deep suspicions that we don't have long to wait for some big news." With this, they ended their talk.

King Hrólf and all his companions became extraordinarily famous from their journey.

Part 7: Concerning the Battle with Skuld, and the Fall of King Hrólf and His Champions

Chapter 47

Now a long time passed while King Hrólf and his champions sat in peace in Denmark, and no one tried to attack them. All of Hrólf's subordinate kings showed him deference and paid their taxes to him, and among them was Hjorvard, Hrólf's brother-in-law.

There came one time when Queen Skuld, Hjorvard's wife, said to him with a heavy sigh, "I don't like paying taxes to King Hrólf on the pain of being tortured by him, and this will go on no longer. You will no longer be his subordinate."

Hjorvard answered, "It would suit us best as it suits others, to endure this and let everything remain quiet."

"You're a little kind of man," she said, "since you want to just put up with every kind of shame that anyone offers you."

He replied, "It isn't possible to fight King Hrólf; no one dares to lift a shield against him."

"You're such a little man, in fact," she said, "that you have no fight in you. Whoever dares nothing, always has nothing. We won't know until we try, how it will or won't go with King Hrólf and his champions. But it so happens, I think, that he'll be the loser of that conflict, and I don't believe it would be too difficult to prove it. Even though he's my relative, that won't protect him from me. He always just sits around at home, because he knows he'll lose a real battle in the open. But if this idea has any chance of success, I'll make up a plan, and I won't leave out any kind of trick that I think might make a difference."

Skuld was the most terrible kind of witch, a descendant of elves on her mother's side, and she would make King Hrólf and his champions know it forcefully. "First I'll send messengers to King Hrólf and ask that he allow me not to pay the taxes I owe him for the next three years on the condition that I'll pay it all in one sum after that. I think this deception will work, and if it does, we'll keep the peace for a time."

Skuld's messengers left on the errand the queen asked them to perform, and King Hrólf did agree to her offer about delayed payment of her taxes.

Chapter 48

At this time Skuld assembled an army of all the strongest men she could find, and most of them were from the worst people of her area. But through her magic and evil deeds, she kept her treachery secret, so that King Hrólf was not aware of it, and none of his champions suspected her plans. Skuld used all of her forbidden magic [seidr] in her efforts to defeat King Hrólf, her own brother, to the point that she sought the company of elves and Norns and uncountable other evil creatures that no natural human could stand against.

For their part, King Hrólf and his champions enjoyed great cheer and entertainments and every kind of game men know about in Lejre, and they did all these things with art and noble manners. Each of them had a concubine for his pleasure.

And now it is told that the army of King Hjorvard and Skuld was ready, and they marched to Lejre with their uncountable troops and arrived at Yuletime. King Hrólf had ordered a great feast for Yule, and his men drank hard during that evening.

Hjorvard and Skuld had their army raise large, long, wonderfully decorated tents outside the city that evening. They had many wagons, all of them full of weapons and armor, though King Hrólf noticed none of this. He was thinking more about his own grandeur and magnanimity and propriety, and about all of the courage that dwelled in his own heart. And he was eager to serve everyone who came, and his good reputation traveled far and wide, and he had every single thing that a king of this world might need to adorn his pride. And it is not told anywhere that King Hrólf or his champions sacrificed to the gods at any time, but rather that they believed in their own strength and abilities. This was because, at the time, the holy faith had not been preached yet here in the Northlands, and thus the men who dwelled in the northern part of the world still had little knowledge of their Creator.

Chapter 49

The next thing to tell of is that Hjalti the Righteous went to the house where his concubine was. He could see clearly that there would be no rest for them under the shadows of the tents of Hjorvard and Skuld. Nonetheless he appeared outwardly calm, and showed no change of mood in his brow when he lay down next to his concubine, the most beautiful of women. And when he had been with her for a time, he shot up to his feet and asked her, "What do you think's better: two twenty-two-year-olds or one eighty-year-old?"

She said, "I think two twenty-two-year-olds would be better than any eighty-year-old man."

"You whore," said Hjalti, "You'll pay for these words." Then he went to her and bit her nose off.

"Let me know if any men start fighting over you now," he said. "But I expect few of them will think you're much of a treasure from here on out."

"You've done evil to me that I didn't deserve," she said.

"I can't be responsible for everything," said Hjalti. Then he took up his weapons, because he saw that all around the city there were armored men and flags set up, and he understood that it would do no good to ignore any longer this hard battle now at hand. He made his way to the hall where King Hrólf and the champions sat, and he said, "Wake up, my lord king, because there is battle to face here at home. There is more need now to fight than to embrace women, and I think that your hall's treasures won't be increased by any further taxes your sister Skuld might pay. She has the ferocity of the Skjoldung family, and I can tell you for a fact that there is an army of no small size outside here with hard swords and other weapons of war, and they are walking around our walls with drawn blades. King Hjorvard must have an unfriendly reason for seeking you out, and after this he will have no more reason to ask you for your kingdom.

"Now is the time," Hjalti continued, "for us to lead the army of our King Hrólf, who refuses us nothing. Let us now do a good job of fulfilling the oaths we swore to defend this most famous of kings who now exists in the Northlands, so that it will be heard of in every land! Let us pay him back for our weapons and armor and so many other gifts—because this isn't going to be just a little bit of farm work. There have been strong hints that this was coming, and we have ignored them for a long time, and I suspect that great events will come after this as well that will be remembered.

"Some might say that I speak out of fear, but it may be that this is the last time King Hrólf will ever drink with his champions and elite guardsmen. Now stand up, all you champions! Say good-bye to your concubines, because another task lies before us now. Make yourselves ready for what comes after this. Up, all you champions, move fast! Get your weapons, all of you!"

Then Hrómund the Hard stood, and Hrólf Fast-hand, and Svipdag and Beigad and Hvítserk the Bold. Haklang stood sixth, and seventh stood Hardrefil; Haki the Brave stood eighth. Strong Vott stood ninth, the tenth to stand was Starólf, and the eleventh was Hjalti the Righteous.

The twelfth to rise was Bodvar Little-bear, who was called this because he had driven all of King Hrólf's berserkers away on account of their arrogance and unfair behavior. Certainly none of them had prevailed against him, and he had killed some of them, because they were like women compared to him when it came to hard tests, even though they had seemed more powerful than he at the time and had possessed the advantage of deception on their side.

This same Bodvar Little-bear stood straight up and put on his armor and said that King Hrólf had need of proud men now—"And heart and spirit alike must work to save the man who now takes his stand alongside King Hrólf!"

Then King Hrólf himself stood and, speaking without fear, he addressed them: "Let us partake of the best drink, and we will drink before we fight and be merry and show them what kind of men King Hrólf's champions are, and we will strive for one thing alone, to let our bold stand live on in memory—for the greatest and the boldest champions of all lands have gathered to me here! Tell Hjorvard and Skuld and their fighters that we will get happily drunk before we receive their 'tribute'!"

It was done as the king said. Skuld's answer to this was as follows: "My brother, King Hrólf, is unlike all others, and it is a greater loss to lose such men, but nonetheless our fate is to fight." King Hrólf was so well regarded that he won praise from his friends and enemies alike.

Chapter 50

Now King Hrólf leapt out of his throne, where he had been drinking alongside all his champions. For now they left the good drink and went outside, all of them except Bodvar Little-bear. They did not see Bodvar and they were perplexed, but they imagined that he had likely either been captured or killed.

As soon as they came outside, a horrible battle began. King Hrólf himself led the standard-bearers forward and his champions alongside him. The rest of his town's army was with him too, not a small amount of men to count, although they amounted to little against their enemies' numbers. In that battle there were great blows to helmets and armor, and many a sword and spear swung in the air, and so many men died that their bodies thatched the earth like a roof.

Hjalti the Righteous said, "Now many a suit of chainmail is ruined, and many weapons are broken, many helmets are split, many riders are knocked dead from their horses. Our king is a man of great spirit, because now he is just as cheerful as he was a little while ago when he was drinking ale as hard as a man can, even though now he fights with both hands. Our king is unlike other kings in battle, because he seems to have the strength of twelve kings. He has killed many a vigorous man, and King Hjorvard can now see that the sword Skofnung bites indeed—that sword crashes loud into their skulls!" It was, in fact, a property of the sword Skofnung that it rang loudly when it hit bone.

It was now a ferociously hard battle, and no one could stand against King Hrólf and his champions. King Hrólf killed so many men with Skofnung that it seemed unbelievable, and so many of King Hjorvard's men fell that they looked as though they were coming down in clumps.

Hjorvard and his men could see that a large bear was going before King Hrólf's men, and the bear was always close to where the king was. With one paw he killed more men than any five of King Hrólf's champions, while swords and arrows alike seemed to bounce off him. This bear broke King Hjorvard's men and horses alike underneath his bulk, and he crushed everything else that was near him with his teeth, until a panicked fear of his approach ran through Hjorvard and Skuld's forces.

Now when Hjalti looked around himself and could not see his comrade Boðvar, he said to King Hrólf, "How can it be that Boðvar is saving himself and coming nowhere near the king, such a great champion as we thought he was, and as he so often proved himself to be?"

King Hrólf said, "He must be somewhere, and I'm sure it's somewhere that benefits us, as long as he has a say in it. Keep up your dignity and keep up your attack, and don't slander him—not any one of you is equal to him. However, I don't mean to scold any of you, because you are all among the most valorous of men."

At this, Hjalti raced home to the king's rooms and saw where Boðvar was sitting and doing nothing. "How long are we going to have to wait for the most famous champion? This is something never known before, that you aren't even standing up on your own feet and testing your strong arms—your arms that are each as strong as a tame bear! Now get up, Boðvar Little-bear, senior man to me in this army, or I will burn down this house and you with it! But the greatest shame is that you are such a great champion, and the king is putting himself in danger for *our* sake, and you are losing all the great praise that you had earlier."

Then Boðvar stood up and snorted and said, "Hjalti, you don't need to try to scare me. I am still unafraid, and I am fully prepared to go. When I was young, I never fled from iron nor from fire. Now I have seldom tested myself against fire, but when it comes to iron, I have always endured it—and I have never failed to stand up to either until now. You say truly that I want to fight very well, and King Hrólf has always called me a champion in front of his men. I have much to repay him, first of all for my marriage to his kinswoman, but also for the twelve farms he has given me, along with many other precious things. It was I who killed Agnar the berserker, who was also a king, and that deed has lived long in the retelling."

Then Boðvar counted up many of the great deeds he had done for Hjalti, and the many men he had killed, and he then asked him to believe that he would also go unafraid to *this* battle, "Though I think this one is much stranger than any we have had before. And you, Hjalti, have not been as helpful to the king in doing this as it seems to you, because by now it would have been decided which side was going to win. But you have been foolish rather than malicious toward our king. And other than the king himself, no one but you would have been the right man to summon me away to the battle—and I would have killed any other. But now it will happen as it is fated to happen, and no counsel will avail. I tell you truly, now in many ways I will give the king less aid than before you called me away from here."

Hjalti said, "It is clear that I am most concerned for you and for King Hrólf. But it is difficult to find the right course in the midst of such strange events."

Chapter 51

After this urging by Hjalti, Bodvar stood up and went out to the battle.

But now the bear disappeared from King Hrólf's troops, and the battle took a turn to the worse for them. Queen Skuld had not been able to get any advantage over them as long as the bear was fighting for King Hrólf. She herself sat in her black tent on a scaffolding that had been set up for her dark magic [*seidr*].

Now the weather changed, as if dark night replaced bright day, and King Hrólf's men saw a terrifying boar coming out of King Hjorvard's army. It was no smaller than a three-year-old steer, and it was a wolfish-gray in color. Arrows flew out of its every whisker, and it killed the bodyguards of King Hrólf, dropping them like the waves of the sea with its monstrous magic.

Now Bodvar Little-bear began to clear a path through the men before him, chopping with both hands. He thought of nothing except to fight as hard as possible, and every man he met fell atop another one. He was bloody up to both of his shoulders, and he was piling up heaps of slaughtered men in every direction around himself, acting in a manner that seemed crazed.

But no matter how many of Skuld's men Bodvar and the rest of Hrólf's champions killed, it was odd to see how their army did not seem to diminish, and all the killing seemed not to reduce their numbers at all, and Hrólf's champions thought they had never seen anything so strange.

Bodvar said, "Skuld's army is huge, and I suspect that their dead are getting revived and raised up again to fight us once more. It will be difficult to fight the undead. As many limbs as we have split, as many shields as we have torn, as many helmets and shirts of chain-mail as we have chopped into small pieces, as many chieftains as we have torn limb from limb—still the undead troops are all the more fearsome, and we do not have the strength to fight them. But now where is that one champion of King Hrólf's, the one who most doubted my courage, and who most often challenged me to duels before I answered him? I don't see him now, though I'm not one to talk behind anyone's back."

Hjalti said, "You speak truly: you're no backbiter. Here stands the man named Hjalti, and you might say I have a little bit of work on my hands. There isn't much distance between you and me right now, and I need the help of good men, foster-brother, because all of my protection has been chopped away. I think I have fought with valor, and though now I can no longer return every blow that is struck at me, I will not defend myself if we are to be guests in Valhalla this evening. Certainly we have never before seen stranger things than we see now, although we have expected the kind of news that we're getting today for a long time."

Bodvar Little-bear said, "Now hear what I tell you: I have fought in twelve great battles, and I have always been called a brave man and I have never shrunk back from any berserker.

"It was I who urged King Hrólf to make his visit to King Adils in his kingdom, and that was a journey where we met with many forms of treachery. But that was nothing next to this current predicament. And now I have been wounded in the heart, so that I cannot be as glad to fight as I have been before. And on an earlier occasion I had already met King Hjorvard, at a time when we happened to cross paths, and neither of us spoke poorly of the other. We had a short fight with weapons at that time; he gave me a blow that nearly killed me, and I cut off his hand and foot. Another blow of mine hit him in the shoulder, and I cut down through his side and into his spine. Yet he did not cry out in response, and only lay down as if he were asleep. I assumed he was dead, but there cannot be many men like him, for he has fought no less bravely since. I have no idea what the source of his power might be.

"Now many men have come against us here, powerful men, and men accorded high honors, and they are falling down upon us from every direction like a snowstorm, so that we can barely raise a shield against them. I do not believe that I recognize Óðin here, but I have a strong feeling of his presence somewhere near, that foul and treacherous son of war! If someone *does* tell me where he's at, I'll beat him like any other low-down vile rodent! That damned poisonous vermin will be badly treated, if I get my hands on him! Who could feel more hate in his heart now than we do, seeing his lord defeated as we watch?"

Hjalti said, "There's no way to bargain with fate, nor to stand against magic."

And in this way their conversation ended.

Chapter 52

King Hrólf defended himself well and manfully, and with greater dignity than any other man had ever shown. His enemies attacked him fiercely, and a circle formed close around him comprised of the select warriors of King Hjorvarð and Skuld.

Now Skuld herself came into the fray, and vigorously encouraged her evil troops to attack King Hrólf. She could see now that his champions were not as close to him anymore, which was what Boðvar Little-bear had mentioned so unhappily, when he said he could not easily help his lord. It was the same for the rest of King Hrólf's champions, for they were just as eager to die with him now as they had been to live with him when they had all been in the prime of their youth.

Now all the king's bodyguards had fallen, and none would stand again. And as for the twelve champions, most had already sustained the injuries that would kill them. This went in the way such things usually go—as the teacher Galterus says, men's strength cannot withstand such devilish power unless God's power is with them. One thing prevented your victory, King Hrólf, that you did not know your Creator.

Now a great storm of magic came upon the champions, so that they fell over on top of one another. Then Hrólf himself emerged from the wall of shields, almost dead of exhaustion.

It does not need to be said in more words than this: King Hrólf fell there, along with all his champions, and they did so with great honor. As for how massive the battle was there, that cannot be explained with mere words. King Hjorvard fell as well, and all his army, except for a few traitors who rose again with Skuld.

Skuld then took the realms of King Hrólf for her own, but she governed them poorly and only a short while.

Moose-Fródi came to avenge his brother Bodvar Little-bear, as he had sworn to do, and King Thórir Dog-foot came as well. This is told in *The Tale of Moose-Fródi*. Moose-Fródi and Thórir received a great deal of support from Queen Yrsa in Sweden, and some men say that it was Vogg who commanded the troops she sent.

They came to Denmark with their army, with Queen Skuld unaware, and they captured her in such a way that none of her magic could be used against them. Then they killed all her evil minions, and they tortured her in various ways.

Then King Hrólf's kingdoms were returned to Hrólf's daughters, and each of the avengers returned to his own home.

As to King Hrólf, he was buried in his mound, and the sword Skofnung was laid inside next to him. Each of his champions was also buried with a weapon. And here ends *The Saga of King Hrólf Kraki and His Champions*.

Appendix

Chapter 1 of *The Saga of Hervor and Heiðrek*, from Hauksbók

A version of *The Saga of Hervor and Heiðrek* is preserved in the manuscript called Hauksbók (ca. AD 1300), which contains some additional material that is not in the best manuscript, designated "R" (see the Introduction for brief notes on the relationships between the manuscripts; the lost, later, manuscript "U" also included similar additional material derived from Hauksbók). While Hauksbók is the oldest physically surviving manuscript that contains this saga, the text in "R" is regarded by scholars as more faithful to the lost original, because the compilers of Hauksbók were notorious for heavily redacting the older sagas and poems copied into that manuscript. So although scholars have not accepted the extra material in Hauksbók as a valid survival of ancient tradition, the alternate beginning to the saga there (especially its expanded origin story for the sword Tyrfing) has a dark but fairy-tale-like quality that may intrigue modern readers.

Below, I have translated Chapter 1 of *The Saga of Hervor and Heiðrek* from scans of the Hauksbók manuscript generously provided by the Árni Magnússon Institute in Reykjavík, Iceland.

* * *

It is told that a very long time ago there was a place called Jotunheimar to the north in Finnmark, south of Ymisland and between there and Hálogaland. There were many giants there at the time, and some of the people there were half-giants. There were close connections between the peoples there, because the giants married women from Ymisland.

Gudmund was the name of the king in Jotunheimar. He was a great maker of sacrifices. He lived at a farm called Grund, in the region of Glasisvellir. He was wise and powerful. He and his men lived for the equivalent of many other men's lives. It was believed that within his kingdom lay the Field of Undying [Ódáinsakr], and that everyone who came there was freed from sickness and old age, and could not die.

After Gudmund died, people began to worship him and call him their god. His son was named Hofund; he was both foresighted and wise, and he was the judge of all the men in the kingdoms nearby. He never pronounced a false judgment, and no one dared to challenge his verdicts or sentences.

Another man was named Hergnír. He was a giant and a dweller in the mountains; he took Áma, daughter of Ymir, from Ymisland, and married her later. Their son was Hergrím the Half-troll, and he took Ogn Elf-work from Jotunheimar and married her later. Their son was Grím.

Starkad, the great daring man of Ála, had been engaged to Ogn earlier. He had eight arms. He had gone north around Elivágar, and took her away to there. Afterward when he came home, he killed Hergrím in a duel. But Ogn killed herself with a sword because she did not want to marry Starkad. After this, Starkad married Álfhild, the daughter of King Álf of the Elf-homes, but Thór killed Starkad. Then Álfhild returned to her people, and Grím the son of Hergrím went with her until he went out raiding. Then he became the greatest kind of warrior, and married Bauggerd, daughter of Starkad. He settled on an island in Hálogaland called Bólm, and he was called Island-Grím of Bólm. The son of Grím and Bauggerd was Arngrím the berserker, who later lived on the island Bólm, and he was the most famous of men.

A king named Sigrlami was said to be the son of Ódin. His own son was named Svafrlami, who took over the kingdom after his father's death and became the greatest kind of warrior.

One day, when King Svafrlami was out hunting, and he was alone without his men, he saw a large stone at about sunset. There were two dwarves by it. Svafrlami enchanted them by means of his beautiful sword, so that they could not return to the stone unless he allowed them. The dwarves begged him to spare their lives. He asked them what their names were, and they told him Dvalin and Dulin.

The king said, "Since you are the most skillful of all dwarves, you must make me the best sword you can. The hilt and the boss must be golden, and the blade must cut through iron as though it were cloth. Rust must never appear on it, and it must claim the victory in every battle and duel for the man who wields it."

The dwarves agreed to his conditions, and the king rode home.

When the appointed day for them to meet again came, Svafrlami returned to the stone. The dwarves were outside, and they handed him the sword, which was very beautiful.

But while Dvalin was standing in the doorway to his stone, he said, "Svafrlami, your sword will be the death of a man each time it is drawn, and it will be used to perform three evil deeds. It will also be your own death."

Then Svafrlami swung at the dwarves with the sword, but they ran into the stone. The sword hit the stone, and the edges sliced into it, but the dwarves escaped through their door into the inner stone.

Svafrlami named the sword Tyrfing, and he always carried it in battles and duels, and always won the victory.

Svafrlami had a daughter named Eyfura, who was the most beautiful of all women and the wisest.

The berserker Arngrím was raiding at this time around Bjarmaland, and he came into the kingdom of King Svafrlami. He had a battle against the king, and the two of them fought personally. Svarfrlami swung Tyrfing at Arngrím, but Arngrím parried with his shield. The sword cut off the bottom of Arngrím's shield, and got stuck in the earth. Then Arngrím cut off Svafrlami's hand, and the sword Tyrfing fell with it. Arngrím killed Svafrlami with it, and then many other men. He left that land with a great amount of loot, and he took Eyfura, the daughter of Svafrlami, with him as well to his home in Bólm. They had twelve sons. Angantýr was the oldest, then Hervarð, then Hjorvarð, Sæming, Hrani, Brami, Barri, Reifnir, Tind, Búi, and the two Haddings. The two Haddings were the youngest and they were twins, and they did only one man's work between them.

Angantýr on his own did two men's work, and he was a head taller than other men. All of the brothers were berserkers, and they were greater than all other men in strength and daring. Even though their numbers might be fewer than their enemies', they were never on a ship with a larger force than just the twelve brothers. They traveled widely to raid and plunder, and they were often victorious in battle, and they became the most famous of men.

Angantýr had the sword Tyrfing, Sæming's sword was Mistilteinn [Mistletoe], and Hervard wielded the sword Broti.

Glossary of Names and Terms:
The Saga of Hervor and Heidrek

Note that the alphabetization of this glossary is based on American rather than Scandinavian conventions. *Æ* is treated as *A+E*, *Đ* is treated as *D*, *Ø* and (in Swedish placenames) *Ö* are treated as *O*, *Q* is printed as and treated as *O*, and *Þ* is printed as and alphabetized as *TH*. The length of vowels is printed but ignored in alphabetization. More details on the anglicization of Old Norse used in this volume can be found in the Introduction.

Names that occur in the lists of descendants in chapters 15–16 are typically excluded, as they have little bearing on the overall understanding of the text. Among the names in chapter 15 are those of the chief characters of *The Saga of Ragnar Lothbrok*, for which see *The Saga of the Volsungs, with The Saga of Ragnar Lothbrok*, translated by Jackson Crawford (Hackett, 2017). The chapter in which a given name or term is first mentioned is enclosed in square brackets. Where the conventional spelling of a name in Old Norse is different from the more anglicized spelling used in the translated narrative, or when an English-language or present-day Scandinavian form of a place-name has been substituted for the Old Norse name, I have indicated the Old Norse spelling in parentheses following the name.

Ægir, also known as *Gymir*; the host of the gods' feasts and a being associated with the sea. He is a giant (or rather, a *jǫtunn*), and in commonplace Norse poetic language, his "daughters" are the waves. [10]

Agnafit, a shore in Sweden from which Hjálmar departs for Samsø. [3]

Alrek (*Alrekr*), called "the Bold" and said to be a ruler among the English. [11]

Andad (*Andaðr*), unknown individual mentioned in the solution to a riddle. [10]

Angantýr (1), a berserker, the oldest son of Angrím who inherits the sword Tyrfing from him. [1]

Angantýr (2), the oldest son of Hervor (1) and Hofund. He is killed in his youth by his brother Heidrek. [5]

Angantýr (3), son of Heidrek and Helga, who becomes king after his father and reclaims the sword Tyrfing from his father's killers. [11]

Árheimar, settlement in southeastern Europe, within the kingdom of Angantýr (3) and apparently his capital. [11]

Arngrím (*Arngrímr*), Viking chieftain who marries Eyfura and inherits the sword Tyrfing from Sigrlami. Their son is Angantýr (1). [1]

Baldr, a famously handsome god and son of Óðin, who was killed through the treacherous plotting of the scheming god Loki. [10]

Berserker (*berserkr*), a type of warrior famous from Norse sagas, myths, and even art, but of uncertain historical reality. The Old Norse word is probably to be interpreted "bear (animal)-shirt," but possibly also "bare shirt." The berserker is said to be a warrior, usually a bully, who goes into a wild frenzy after biting his shield, but who is extremely fatigued after the frenzy passes. Berserkers are often impervious to fire and/or iron, and their powers are said to be the gift of the god Óðin. Berserkers are typically seen either singly or in groups of twelve (as with Angantýr (1) and his brothers). [1]

Bjarmar (*Bjarmarr*), a jarl, and the maternal grandfather of Hervor (1) who raises her. [2]

Bólm (*Bólmr*), island home of Arngrím and birthplace of Angantýr (1). [1]

Carpathian Mountains, a mountain range in southeastern Europe. The Old Norse term used in the saga, *Hervaðafjǫll,* "*Hervaða*-mountains," is apparently an extremely archaic borrowing from Greek or another language of that region, showing the sound change known as Grimm's Law, which had occurred in the Proto-Germanic language (ancestral to Old Norse) much more than a thousand years before the saga was written. [11]

Delling (*Dellingr*), a name that occurs in some lists of dwarf names, as well as in *Vafthrúdnismál* in the *Poetic Edda* as the name of the father of *Dagr* "Day," and in *Hávamál* (st. 160; see *The Wanderer's Hávamál*). The words *fyr Dellings durum* "before Delling's doors" also occur in five of the riddles Óðin poses to King Heidrek in chapter 10. [10]

Denmark (*Danmǫrk*), roughly coterminous with the modern country, but in the medieval period it included much of what is now southern Sweden. [15]

Dísir, plural designation for supernatural creatures that might have been minor goddesses of home and hearth, or spirit-like beings that protected certain families. [7]

Dnieper (*Danpar*), a river in southeastern Europe. [11]

Dúnheid (*Dúnheiðr*), site of the battle between Angantýr (3) and Hlod. [13]

Dvalin (*Dvalinn*), a typical name for a dwarf. Hervor (1) calls the sword Tyrfing "that sword that Dvalin made" in the poem *The Waking of Angantýr* in chapter 4, though she may use this expression merely as a poetic way of saying "that sword that a dwarf made." [4]

Dwarf (*dvergr*), a mythical, humanlike creature. Dwarves are represented as master craftsmen, and many of them have shape-changing abilities (for instance, Andvari lives as a fish and Otter as an otter in *The Saga of the Volsungs*) and the power to enter solid stone in order to hide themselves. [1]

England (in Old Norse also *England*), roughly coterminous with the modern country in Great Britain, though it was not one unified kingdom during the early Middle Ages. [9]

Eyfura, daughter of Sigrlami, wife of Arngrím, and mother of Angantýr (1). [1]

Foreigners, a term used, capitalized, in this translation to render Old Norse *Valar*. The Old Norse word is related to the English word *Welsh*, and must have come from a Proto-Germanic word that designated a foreign people. For the early English, the quintessential foreigners were the Welsh, while in Norse literature this term generally denotes French-speaking peoples. However, the poem *The Battle of the Goths and Huns* in which the term occurs is very archaic, and "Romans" is not an unthinkable translation in that context, especially given that their ruler is named as *Kjár*, a derivation from *Caesar* (which of course was also a title used by rulers of the medieval Holy Roman Empire in France and Germany, among many other pretenders to Roman greatness in the following centuries). [11]

Fródmar (*Fróðmarr*) (1), a name Hervor seems to use as a (typical?) slave's name when insulting what she thinks is her slave father. [4]

Fródmar (*Fróðmarr*) (2), a jarl in England who fosters Hervor (2). [9]

Geats, adapted from Old English as a translation of Old Norse *Gautar*, the people of Götaland. [11]

Gestumblindi, an enemy of Heiðrek who sacrifices to Óðin and asks him to take his place in Heiðrek's court. Óðin goes to Heiðrek, disguised as Gestumblindi, and proposes riddles to him in chapter 10. [10]

Gizur (*Gizurr*) (1), called "the Old," the foster-father of Angantýr (3). [5]

Gizur (*Gizurr*) (2), mentioned as a king of Götaland. [11]

Glasisvellir, lands of King Guðmund and later of his son King Hofund. [4]

Götaland (*Gautland*), a region of modern Sweden that was once politically distinct from Sweden proper; in Old English its people were called "Geats" (Bēowulf, famously, was a Geat). *Götaland* is the Swedish spelling that can be found on modern maps. [15]

Goths (*gotar*), a Germanic people of late antiquity and the early Middle Ages. Beginning in chapter 11, the people of Angantýr (3) are identified as Goths. [11]

Graf River (*Grafá*), a river mentioned in chapter 11. While the geography of the saga is vague and as often points toward southeastern Europe as to Scandinavia, there is a river in Nord-Trøndelag, Norway called *Gravåa*, the Modern Norwegian cognate of this name, and the river does empty into a lake as described in the saga. [11]

Grýtings (*Grýtingar*), a Gothic tribe to which Gizur (2) belongs. [12]

Guðmund (*Guðmundr*), king in Glasisvellir. [4]

Hadding (*Haddingr*), a name shared by two brothers, both berserkers, and the fifth and sixth sons of Angrím. [1]

Harald (*Haraldr*), aged ruler of Reiðgotaland. [6]

Heiðrek (*Heiðrekr*), the younger son of Hervor (1), who begins as an ill-tempered youth who accidentally kills his brother Angantýr (2) and then is given the sword Tyrfing by his mother after his father banishes him for the crime. Eventually he becomes a powerful king in his own right. [4]

Heiðrek Wolf-skin (*Heiðrekr úlfhamr*), son of Angantýr (3). [15]

Hel, the underworld to which most people are committed for the afterlife. According to the classic understanding of Norse mythology, men who die in battle go to Valhalla instead, but in fact the Norse conception of the afterlife seems to have been very vague. Especially in archaic poems, Hel may also mean simply "the grave," as it seems to in the poem *The Waking of Angantýr* in chapter 4. [4]

Helga, first wife of Heiđrek, and daughter of Harald. She is the mother of Angantýr (3). She kills herself after her husband kills her father in battle. [6]

Hervard (*Hervarðr*) **(1),** a berserker, the third son of Angrím. [1]

Hervard (*Hervarðr*) **(2),** a man's name assumed by Hervor (1) when she departs for Samsø in disguise. [4]

Hervor (*Hervǫr*) **(1),** daughter of Angantýr (1) and Sváva. She grows up in the lands of her maternal grandfather Bjarmar before leaving for Samsø (disguised as a man, under the name Hervard) to retrieve the sword Tyrfing from her father's grave mound. [4]

Hervor (*Hervǫr*) **(2),** daughter of Heiđrek with his unnamed third wife. Like her grandmother, Hervor (1), Hervor (2) is a shieldmaiden. [9]

Hjálmar (*Hjálmarr*), known as "the Bold." He is a warrior in the service of King Ingjald, and fights a duel against Hjorvarđ and his brothers on Samsø to contest Hjorvarđ's proposal to marry Ingjald's daughter Ingibjorg. "Hjálmar's killer" or "killer of Hjálmar" is a poetic way of referring to the sword Tyrfing. [2]

Hjorvard (*Hjǫrvarðr*), a berserker, the second son of Angrím. He swears to marry Ingibjorg. [1]

Hlod (*Hlǫðr*), son of Heiđrek and Sifka. He grows up with his mother's people in Hunland, fostered by his maternal grandfather King Humli. [7]

Hnefatafl, a Norse board game similar to chess, but with one side limited to defensive actions and the other to offense. Note that the board game in ch. 5 is specifically referred to as "chess" (*skáktafl*), not *hnefatafl*. [10]

Hofund (*Hǫfundr*), son of Guđmund, who marries Hervor (1). [5]

Hrani, a berserker, the fourth son of Angrím. [1]

Humli, king in Hunland. [7]

Hunland, a mythical kingdom. The Huns were an Asian people of late antiquity and the early Middle Ages whose raids in Europe reached their peak in the fifth century AD and brought them into both conflicts and alliances with the Goths and other Germanic peoples. Numerous human characters in the Norse sagas are referred to as Huns. [7]

Ingibjorg (*Ingibjǫrg*), daughter of Ingjald, for whose hand in marriage Hjálmar (with Odd) fights Hjorvarđ (with his brothers). She is not named in the saga until Hjálmar's death poem. [3]

Ingjald (*Ingjaldr*), a king in Sweden. [2]

Ítrek (*Ítrekr*), unknown individual mentioned in the solution to a riddle. [10]

Jarl, Norse title for a powerful nobleman. [2]

Jassar Mountains (*Jassarfjǫll*), an unknown range, apparently in southeastern Europe. [13]

Kjár (*Kjárr*), a name likely derived from the title *Caesar*. [11]

Mirkwood (*Myrkviðr*), a famous forest mentioned in several poems and sagas of human heroes. It is associated vaguely with "the south" and with the Goths. [11]

Munarvág (*Munarvágr*), Old Norse name for an unknown harbor on the Danish island of Samsø (possibly in its south, based on a vague hint in Bjarmar's response to Hervor (1) in chapter 4). It is also a setting in *The Saga of Ragnar Lothbrok*. [3]

Mǫrk, a monetary unit, based on the weight of the precious metal involved, of the Norse Middle Ages. [6]

Norn, one of the female beings who determine the fate of gods and mortals. [14]

Norway (*Noregr*), roughly coterminous with the modern country, but it is a region of small independent chiefdoms, rather than a unified nation, in the early Middle Ages. [15]

Odd (*Oddr*), known as "the Traveler" or more often as "Arrow-Odd" (*Ǫrvar-Oddr*). He is the hero of his own long saga (*Ǫrvar-Odds saga* or "Arrow-Odd's Saga"), and appears in *The Saga of Hervor and Heidrek* as a companion in arms to Hjálmar during his fight on Samsø against Hjorvard and Angantýr. He wears a silk shirt that is impervious to weapons. [3]

Ódin (*Óðinn*), a god associated with poetry and war. He is often portrayed as a shrewd figure pursuing his own selfish interests, including the dispatching of human warriors so that they may join his army in Valhalla (the "hall of the slain" where his Valkyries bring dead warriors). Ódin is very frequently seen in disguise and takes many names, but even in disguise he is usually recognizable to the reader as an old man with one eye, often dressed in a gray or blue cloak and a wide-brimmed hat. [3]

Ormar (*Ormarr*), foster-father of Hervor (2). [13]

Reidgotaland (*Reiðgotaland*), lands ruled by Harald and later Heidrek and Angantýr (3). The location at times seems vaguely within Scandinavia and other times (especially in chapters 11–14 and the poetry within them) to be in southeastern Europe along the Dnieper. [6]

Rus, a term for the people of an early medieval Swedish tribe, or the Slavic people of the kingdoms they founded in modern Russia and Ukraine. The word appears in this volume in translating *Gardaríki*, an Old Norse term for the Rus kingdoms, and *Gardakonungr*, the king of these regions. [1]

Samsø (*Sámsey*), a small island in Denmark where Hjálmar (with Odd) fights Hjorvard and Angantýr (1) (with their brothers) and where Angantýr and the other combatants are later buried. The island seems to have had a special association with magic, as it is also mentioned as a place where Ódin practiced magic in the poem *Lokasenna* in the Poetic Edda, and where a talking wooden idol is encountered at the end of *The Saga of Ragnar Lothbrok*. [2]

Saxony (*Saxland*), a region and former independent kingdom in Germany, corresponding to the northern rather than eastern region with that name today. [8]

Sifka, daughter of Humli and concubine of Heidrek. She cohabitates with Heidrek before and after his second marriage, and she is the mother with him of Hlod. Heidrek kills Sifka before his third marriage. [7]

Shieldmaiden (*skjaldmær*), Norse designation for a woman who fights in battles. [9]

Sigrlami, Rus king and original owner of the sword Tyrfing. [1]

Sleipnir, the eight-legged horse of Ódin. [10]

Sóti, a place where Hjálmar recollects fighting. [3]

Sváva, wife of Angantýr (1) and mother of Hervor (1). [2]

Sweden (*Svíþjóð*), in the Middle Ages, refers chiefly to the eastern part of the modern country centered around Uppsala. Much of the southern part of what is now Sweden belonged to Denmark until early modern times, and in the early medieval period Götaland was also a distinct kingdom. [3]

Tyrfing (*Tyrfingr*), a sword, famously unable to be resheathed until it had drawn a man's blood. [1]

Valdar (*Valdarr*), mentioned as a king of Denmark. [11]

Valhalla (*Valhǫll*), hall of Ódin, where men who die in battle are said to reside. [3]

Yule, translation used in this volume for Old Norse *jól*, a holiday held at approximately the winter solstice. Oaths sworn on Yule Eve were considered especially binding. [2]

Glossary of Names and Terms:
The Saga of Hrólf Kraki and His Champions

Note that the alphabetization of this glossary is based on American rather than Scandinavian conventions. *Æ* is treated as *A+E*, *Ð* is treated as *D*, *Ø* and (in Swedish placenames) *Ö* are treated as *O*, *Q* is printed as and treated as *O*, and *Þ* is printed as and alphabetized as *TH*. The length of vowels is printed but ignored in alphabetization. More details on the anglicization of Old Norse used in this volume can be found in the Introduction. The chapter in which a given name or term is first mentioned is enclosed in square brackets. Where the conventional spelling of a name in Old Norse is different from the more anglicized spelling used in the translated narrative, or when an English-language or present-day Scandinavian form of a place-name has been substituted for the Old Norse name, I have indicated the Old Norse spelling in parentheses following the name.

Adils, a Swedish king who marries King Helgi's daughter and former wife Yrsa after Yrsa divorces her father. [14]

Agnar (*Agnarr*) (1), son of Hróar and Ogn. [12]

Agnar (*Agnarr*) (2), a berserker that Bodvar alludes to killing, though the story is not told in the saga. [50]

Beigad (*Beigaðr*), a son of Svip and brother of Svipdag. He assists his brother Svipdag in the battle in which Svipdag is maimed fighting for King Adils of Sweden, and then follows Svipdag when he joins the champions of King Hrólf of Denmark. [18]

Bera, daughter of a wealthy farmer and lover of Bjorn. Her name means "(female) bear." [25]

Berserker (*berserkr*), a type of warrior famous from Norse sagas, myths, and even art, but of uncertain historical reality. The Old Norse word is *berserkr*, probably to be interpreted "bear (animal)-shirt," but possibly also "bare shirt." The berserker is said to be a warrior, usually a bully, who goes into a wild frenzy after biting his shield, but who is extremely fatigued after the frenzy passes. Berserkers are often impervious to fire and/or iron, and their powers are said to be the gift of the god Óđin. Berserkers are typically seen either singly or in groups of twelve. [16]

Bjálki, a warrior in the service of King Hrólf of Denmark. [22]

Bjorn (*Bjǫrn*), son of Hring. He is cursed to spend his days as a bear by his stepmother Hvít after he refuses her advances. His name means "(male) bear." [24]

Bodvar (*Bǫđvarr*), third of the three sons of Bjorn and Bera. He is often called Bodvar *Bjarki* "Little-bear." In his adulthood he becomes a great hero in the court of King Hrólf Kraki and marries Hrólf's daughter Drífa. In his final battle in the saga, it seems that he takes the form of a bear as his father once had. [26]

Denmark (*Danmǫrk*), roughly coterminous with the modern country, but in the medieval period it included much of what is now southern Sweden. [1]

Drífa, daughter of King Hrólf of Denmark. She is married to Bodvar after he joins Hrólf's court. Another daughter, Skúr, is mentioned in ch. 22, but never again, and Drífa is called "the king's only daughter" when she is next mentioned in ch. 37. [22]

Elf (*álfr*), a creature described only in the vaguest terms in Norse mythology. Elves seem to have human-like appearance but also a strong association with magic and (sometimes) the pagan gods. In some contexts, though not in this saga, they seem to be much the same kind of creature as dwarves. [15]

Finnmark (*Finnmǫrk*), region in far northern Norway, above the Arctic Circle. [24]

Fródi (*Fróđi*), an early Danish king, and brother of Hálfdan (in Snorri Sturluson's *Prose Edda,* though never in the saga, their father is identified as Friđleif). He invades his brother Hálfdan's territory and kills him. He dies when his hall is burned by his nephews Helgi and Hróar. [1]

Fýrisvellir, a valley, or town within that valley, in the vicinity of Uppsala. As King Hrólf and his champions ride out of Uppsala in chapter 45, King Hrólf strews his path through the valley with gold to slow down the pursuing Swedes. [45]

Galterus, a "teacher" alluded to by the narrator in chapter 52 when he castigates King Hrólf and his men for failing to know about the Christian God. As this is a Latinized form of the name *Walter,* the specific medieval Christian writer alluded to is uncertain. [52]

Götaland (*Gautland*), a region of modern Sweden that was once politically distinct from Sweden proper; in Old English its people were called "Geats" (Bēowulf, famously, was a Geat). *Götaland* is the Swedish spelling that can be found on modern maps. [29]

Gram (*Gramr*), the dog of King Hrólf. [43]

Gullinhjalti, a sword of King Hrólf's that he gives to Hjalti, and the source of Hjalti's name (*Hjalti* means "hilt"; *Gullinhjalti*, "golden hilt"). [36]

Hábrók, the hawk of King Hrólf. He kills the hawks of Adils during the battle in chapter 44. [40]

Haki the Brave (*Haki inn frøkni*), one of King Hrólf's champions, named only during Hrólf's final fight. Possibly to be identified with an equally obscure Haki named as a champion in chapter 25 of *The Saga of the Volsungs*. [49]

Haklang (*Haklangr*), one of King Hrólf's champions, named only during Hrólf's final fight. [49]

Hálfdan, an early Danish king, brother of Fródi (in Snorri Sturluson's *Prose Edda,* though never in the saga, their father is identified as Fridleif). He is the father of Hróar, Helgi, and Signý. He is killed in an invasion by his brother Fródi. [1]

Ham (*Hamr*), false name assumed by Helgi when he and his brother seek protection from Sævil. [3]

Hardrefil (*Harðrefill*), one of King Hrólf's champions, named only during Hrólf's final fight. [49]

Heid (*Heiðr*), a seeress or witch (Old Norse *vǫlva*) who attends a feast hosted by Fródi for Sævil. She hints that Hróar and Helgi are still alive. [3]

Hel, the underworld to which most people are committed for the afterlife. According to the classic understanding of Norse mythology, men who die in battle go to Valhalla instead, but in fact the Norse conception of the afterlife seems to have been very vague. Especially in archaic poems, Hel may also mean simply "the grave." [5]

Helgi, son of Hálfdan. After his father's murder by Fródi, he escapes to Vífil's island with his brother Hróar and later to the home of his brother-in-law Sævil, eventually burning his uncle Fródi's hall down during a feast. As an adult he becomes king of Denmark, rapes Queen Ólof of Saxony after she refuses to marry him, producing his daughter Yrsa, and he has a son, Hrólf, with Yrsa before he knows she is his daughter. After Yrsa leaves him and marries King Adils of Sweden, Helgi visits her there and is killed in an ambush by Adils's men. [4]

Hjalti, name assumed by Hott after he drinks a monster's blood and becomes a champion of King Hrólf's. The name, which means "hilt," is based on the name of the sword King Hrólf gives him, *Gullinhjalti* ("golden hilt"). He is nicknamed "Hjalti the Righteous" (*Hjalti inn hugprúði*) by King Hrólf because as a hero of his court he does not avenge the harms done to him as a child by the senior warriors there. [36]

Hjorvard (*Hjǫrvarðr*), a king married to King Hrólf's half-sister Skuld. Hrólf treats him as a subordinate ruler, which frustrates him into rebellion. [23]

Hó, one of Vífil's dogs. Hróar and Helgi take the dogs' names when they are hiding from Fródi on Vífil's island. [1]

Hopp (*Hoppr*), one of Vífil's dogs. Hróar and Helgi take the dogs' names when they are hiding from Fródi on Vífil's island. [1]

Hott (*Hǫttr*), original name of Hjalti before Bodvar makes him drink a monster's blood and he becomes more courageous. [33]

Hrani (1), false name assumed by Hróar when he and his brother seek protection from Sævil. [3]

Hrani (2), false name assumed by Ódin when he hosts King Hrólf and his army three times on their expedition to Uppsala. [39]

Hring (*Hringr*), the king of Uppdalir. [24]

Hróar (*Hróarr*), son of Hálfdan. After his father's murder by Fródi, he escapes to Vífil's island with his brother Helgi and later to the home of his brother-in-law Sævil, eventually burning Fródi's hall down during a feast. He later becomes King of Northumberland in England. [1]

Hrók (*Hrókr*), son of Sævil. He kills Hróar after Hróar cuts his feet off for throwing a ring into the ocean. [6]

Hrólf (*Hrólfr*), son of King Helgi and his daughter Yrsa. He becomes King of Denmark after the death of his father Helgi. [12]

Hrólf Fast-hand (*Hrólfr skjóthendi*), one of King Hrólf's champions, named only during Hrólf's final fight. [49]

Hrómund the Hard (*Hrómundr harði*), one of King Hrólf's champions, named only during Hrólf's final fight. [49]

Hvít, daughter of Ingibjorg and the unnamed king of the Sámi. She marries Hring and unsuccessfully tries to seduce his son Bjorn before cursing him to turn into a bear. [24]

Hvítserk the Bold (*Hvítserkr inn hvati*), oldest son of Svip (and brother of Svipdag). He assists his brother Svipdag in the battle in which Svipdag is maimed fighting for King Aðils of Sweden, and then follows Svipdag when he joins the champions of King Hrólf of Denmark. [18]

Ingibjorg (*Ingibjǫrg*), mother of Hvít. [24]

Jarl, Norse title for a powerful nobleman. [1]

Lejre (*Hleiðargarðr*), capital of King Hrólf of Denmark. *Lejre* is the site's name in Modern Danish. [23]

Lund (*Lundr*), a city that lies today in extreme southern Sweden, but historically was a major city and sometime capital of the Kingdom of Denmark (in pre-modern times when that kingdom extended into the Scandinavian peninsula and claimed the southernmost part of what is now Sweden). [3]

Moose-Fródi (*Elg-Fróði*), oldest of the three sons of Bjorn and Bera (curiously, Bjorn foretells in ch. 26 that Elg-Fróði will be their second-born). His top half is that of a man, but he is a moose from the navel down. In his adulthood he becomes a fearsome road agent, but remains loyal to his brothers. It is unclear if he is to be pictured as centaur-like (with a moose-like figure and four moose-legs) or satyr-like (with a humanoid figure, but with two legs that resemble a moose's). The first element in his name in Old Norse, *elg-*, is related to the English word "elk," but this means "moose" in Scandinavia (as well as in British English). [26]

Naming-gift (*nafnfestr*), a gift given along with a name. It was traditional in Norse society for a father to give a newborn a gift when he named it, and in the sagas men also often demand a gift from someone who gives them a nickname, perhaps with tongue in cheek. [42]

Nordri (*Norðri*), king "over a certain part of England" (later identified as Northumberland) and father of Ogn. [6]

Norn, one of the female beings who determine the fate of gods and mortals. [48]

Northlands, translation used in this volume for Old Norse *Norðrlǫnd* (literally, "Northlands"; translated as "Scandinavia" in *The Saga of the Volsungs with the Saga of Ragnar Lothbrok*). [7]

Norway (*Noregr*), roughly coterminous with the modern country, but it is a region of small independent chiefdoms, rather than a unified nation, in the early Middle Ages. [24]

Ogn (*Ǫgn*), daughter of Norðri and wife of Hróar. [6]

Óðin (*Óðinn*), a god associated with poetry and war. He is often portrayed as a shrewd figure pursuing his own selfish interests, including the dispatching of human warriors so that they may join his army in Valhalla (the "hall of the slain" where his Valkyries bring dead warriors). Óðin is very frequently seen in disguise and takes many names, but even in disguise he is usually recognizable to the reader as an old man with one eye, often dressed in a gray or blue cloak and a wide-brimmed hat. [46]

Ólof (*Ólǫf*), warlike queen of Saxony. She is raped by Helgi after she refuses to marry him, and their daughter is Yrsa. [7]

Regin (*Reginn*), foster-father of Helgi and Hróar who helps them escape from King Fróði after the death of their father, Hálfdan. He later helps them escape from Fróði's hall during the feast for Sævil in which the seeress Heið hints that they are alive. [1]

Sævil (*Sævill*), a jarl, and husband of Signý. [1]

Sámi (*Finnar*), indigenous people of northern Scandinavia, unrelated by customs or language to the Norse-speaking (or later Norwegian- and Swedish-speaking) peoples. In Old Norse literature they are often portrayed as masters of magic. [24]

Saxony (*Saxland*), a region and former independent kingdom in Germany, corresponding to the northern rather than eastern region with that name today. [7]

Seiðhjallr, "scaffold" for *seiðr* (dark magic), a tool used by a *vǫlva* or sorceress here and in other sagas. [3]

Seiðr, Old Norse term for a type of magic, always regarded as evil when practiced by men, and often when practiced by women. *Seiðr* magic seems especially concerned with seeing the future and with causing indirect harm to others. [51]

Signý, daughter of Hálfdan, and wife of Sævil. [1]

Sigríd (*Sigríðr*), the mother of Helgi and Hróar and by implication Hálfdan's wife, though she is only mentioned by name when she burns to death along with Fróði. [5]

Skjoldungs (*Skjǫldungar*), the legendary dynasty of Danish kings to which Hálfdan, Helgi, Hrólf, etc. belong. They are named for Skjold, the grandfather of Hálfdan and Fróði (who is nowhere named in the saga, but whose name is known from e.g., Snorri Sturluson's *Prose Edda*). [3]

Skofnung (*Skǫfnungr*), the sword of King Hrólf. [45]

Skuld, a witch, daughter of King Helgi and an unnamed "elf-woman." She marries Hjorvard and encourages his rebellion against her brother, King Hrólf. [15]

Skúr, daughter of King Hrólf of Denmark. She is mentioned alongside Drífa when they are both introduced in ch. 22, but Skúr is never mentioned again, and in ch. 37 Drífa is called "the king's only daughter." [22]

Sleep-thorn (*svefnþorn*), a never-described magical item that seems to be, quite simply, some kind of thorn that causes sleep when it pricks a person. A "sleep-thorn" is mentioned in the *Volsungs* legends as well, as when Óðin stings his Valkyrie Brynhild with one before imprisoning her in her burning ring of fire. [7]

Starólf (*Starólfr*), one of King Hrólf's champions, named only during Hrólf's final fight. [49]

Svíagrís (*Svíagríss*), a ring especially prized by King Aðils, later given by his wife Yrsa to her son King Hrólf. [44]

Svip (*Svipr*), a Swedish farmer. [18]

Svipdag (*Svipdagr*), a son of Svip. After killing four of the berserkers of King Aðils, he takes their place an elite war leader at Aðils's court but quits this position when Aðils fails to come to his aid in a great battle where he is severely maimed. He later goes into the service of King Hrólf. [18]

The Tale of Moose-Fródi (Elg-Fróða þáttr), apparently a "sequel" of sorts in which the story of Moose-Fródi taking vengeance for his brother Boðvar was told. The story is lost. [52]

Thórir Dog-foot (*Þórir hundsfótr*), second of the three sons of Bjorn and Bera (curiously, Bjorn foretells in ch. 26 that Thórir will be their first-born). He has a generally human figure but his feet look like those of a dog. In his adulthood he becomes king of Götaland. [26]

Troll (Old Norse *troll* or *trǫll*), vague term for a threatening humanoid being, sometimes simply a human with magical powers, an ugly appearance, or an evil disposition, but more often a threatening non-human monster. [35]

Uppdalir, historical (mythical?) region of uncertain location in Norway. [24]

Uppsala (*Uppsalir*), medieval capital of Sweden. [14]

Valhalla (*Valhǫll*), hall of Óðin, where men who die in battle are said to reside. [51]

Valsleit (*Valsleitr*), a jarl in Uppdalir who marries Bera after her sons are grown. [30]

Var (*Varr*), the name of both of the skilled craftsmen who work for Fródi. [5]

Vífil (*Vífill*), a friend of Hálfdan who lives on his own small island where he hides Hálfdan's sons Helgi and Hróar after Hálfdan's death. [1]

Vogg (*Vǫggr*), a low-ranking servant of Queen Yrsa who inadvertently gives King Hrólf his nickname (*kraki* or "pole-ladder" from the shape of his face), and then pledges to avenge the king in exchange for his gift of a golden ring. [42]

Volund (*Vǫlundr*), identified as an elf, a mythical smith of great talent. Fródi's great craftsmen are compared to him in talent. [5]

Volva (*vǫlva*), "seeress" or "witch," the practitioner of *seiðr* magic. [3]

Vott (*Vǫttr*), one of King Hrólf's champions, named only during Hrólf's final fight. [49]

Yrsa, daughter of Helgi and Ólof. She is despised by her mother because of her origin (she is the result of Helgi's raping of Ólof), and thus grows up among poor farmers and is assigned to do menial tasks such as sheepherding. However, Helgi falls in love with her (not realizing she is his daughter) and marries her. [9]

Yule, translation used in this volume for Old Norse *jól*, a holiday held at approximately the winter solstice. [15]